The Quilting Cruise

Miranda Hathaway Adventure #9

___

Mary Devlin Lynch
and
Beth Devlin-Keune

© 2020 Mary Devlin Lynch/Beth Devlin-Keune
All rights reserved
Published by *DevlinsBooks*

ISBN: 9798665350622

**This book is dedicated to best friends.
The ones who accept you, love you, challenge you, and make life better.
If you're lucky like me, you get a sibling who is also a best friend.
Hold on. Keep calling. Send a card. Ask them if they're okay. Don't let them slip away.
So to all the Miranda's who have a wacky Diane to make them more,
to challenge them and make them laugh, and to all the Dianes who have a calm,
thoughtful, grounding Miranda...
Be grateful and honor them. Love is rare.
We are so Blessed.
Beth**

Contact Information:
    E-mail: devlinsbooks@gmail.com
    Facebook: devlinsbooks
    Twitter: @devlinsbooks
    Blog: www.devlinsbooks.com

I don't want to go on a cruise ship. I don't suffer motion sickness but have realized along the way that I do have an unreasonable fear of water, big water, endless water, water stretching to the horizon especially.

But, after Queenie, President of our Cutler Quilt Guild #1, and Sarah, our most senior quilter, went on a cruise a few months ago, they were excited for us all to go on one. They've talked about it off and on and then, last week, they handed out brochures! They asked us all to think about it. I said nothing because it didn't require a great deal of thought on my part.

Now, during our weekly meeting, as we headed over to the cutting table in Queenie's shop for our coffee and donuts break, I could tell they were about to bring it up.

I tried a pre-emptive strike. "Hey, how about a guild trip to Las Vegas? There's a quilt conference there in early July!" I said with enthusiasm.

Dead silence followed as everyone stared at me. Even Gabe, my husband, who had come out of the office where he ran the long arm machine, seemed surprised.

"Miranda, don't you want to go on the quilting cruise?" Queenie asked in amazement. "It's a cruise! And it's a Quilting Cruise! And it's the Bahamas, for heaven's sake."

"Let her explain, Queenie. Give her a chance." Sarah patted my arm. "Tell us what your problem is, honey."

"The water." It came out as more of a whisper than I intended.

Judy, quickly swallowing a bite of her donut, spoke up first. "Can you give us more than that? Most cruises take place on water."

I felt my face pink up. "I'm afraid of water, you know, not bath or shower water but," I spread my arms wide, "'no land in sight' water."

"Wow." Judy sighed as she reached for another donut. "Okay then, there's no getting around that, is there?"

Helping to break the awkward moment, Brittany, a pixie brunette and mother of three, put down her coffee and spoke up.

"Well, I don't think I can go, either. I'd love to go, I really would. And I'm not gonna lie, John and both of our families offered to arrange a schedule for the kids for the week." She smiled ruefully. "But Braxton's only eleven months old. I don't think I can leave him for that long."

We all nodded our understanding. I still remember vividly the first time I left Zoey with my in-laws, alternating between fretting and calling home repeatedly.

"Of course not." Sarah said gently.

"Fair enough." Judy added.

After another awkward moment, Queenie cleared her throat. "So I'll sign us up. That would be me, Sarah, Judy, Shelby, right? Is it okay to share two rooms? Or do you want singles?"

"If it's cheaper, I'm good with sharing." Shelby piped up.

Sarah smiled. "Don't worry, honey, I've got this. Consider it a small graduation gift."

The girl's eyes lit up. "Really? Are you sure it's not too much?"

Shelby, our newest quilter, was working part-time at a salon while finishing up cosmetology school. She had come to Cutler over a year ago. It seemed that her mother and stepfather down south were using her as a free babysitter for her four younger siblings and as a free housemaid.

So her aunt and uncle "rescued" her, bringing her to Cutler to work in their shop, Danny's Donuts, and take care of their kids. It didn't seem like much of an upgrade to us. We mistakenly thought that Shelby might be the mother of the baby Harry found at Christmas and, well, long story short, we wanted to make it up to her. To our surprise, we found that the chubby, sullen girl with the bad complexion and stringy hair wanted to be a beautician or a cosmetologist. We got her a part-time job at a local salon, working for free as training. Now she was a paid employee and taking classes at the community college, very popular with the younger customers. She was a Cutler girl now enjoying a real rescue.

Sarah had taken a special interest in her and was providing free room and board at the large Victorian where she had been living alone since the death of her twin sister, Harriet, last year. The situation suited them both and, I must say, we were all relieved that Sarah had the company.

Sarah waved her off. "It's fine. You deserve a break; you've been working hard."

Judy grinned at Shelby, who was about the same age as her boy Tommy. "Why don't we let Queenie and Sarah continue their cruising together and we'll bunk up if that's okay with you?"

Shelby nodded eagerly. "Cool."

We finished our break and completed the rest of the quilt guild meeting working on our own projects and talking about other things. Still, I left feeling as if I'd let them down.

On the way home, Gabe ventured, "I had no idea you were afraid of water."

I managed a grin and a shrug. "I'm not afraid of water; I'm afraid of *drowning*."

My husband humored me with a chuckle. "So I gather you don't swim?"

I shivered. "Oh, no."

"This is a whole new side of you," he teased.

"Make fun if you must but I simply never wanted to swim or go in the water, period." I sighed. "I know the cruise would be wonderful. I just don't think I can do it."

He reached over and patted my hand. "There will be other road trips with the quilters, honey. You don't have to go."

Two

"You have to go!" Diane, my BFF, yelled at me over the phone.

I raised an eyebrow. "Really?"

"Yes. If you don't go, I can't go!"

"You're not listening, Dee. I don't want to go."

"No, seriously," she went on, ignoring me. "School will be out by then and I know I can swing it."

"Well, I'm happy for you."

"Psshaww. It's all in your mind. I'll put a glass of wine in your hand and we'll stay inside mostly and you'll be fine."

I stayed silent.

"Puh-leeze, Mandy. I so need this. You have no idea what high school kids are like. I need a VACATION!"

"You and Mark go away every year."

She lowered her voice. "A vacation with Mark is like being at home but with a camera and sunburn. It's just not…exciting."

"Wow, you are stressed. You adore Mark."

"Of course I do. But he doesn't have a knack for adventure like you do."

I could almost see the lightbulb going off over her head. "Hey, you do know that the boat spends a lot of time docked, right? From what I heard, there are stops like every other day for shopping and sightseeing and stuff."

I sighed loudly into the phone. "I'll think about it."

"Yaaayy." She squealed, knowing she had me.

I clicked off the call. At that moment, I felt that if I needed a vacation from anyone, it was Diane. I looked down to see Harry staring up at me with his big green eyes narrowed. He shook his head (I swear), clicked a couple of times, and walked away in disgust.

Let me introduce you to Harry who, yes, bears the same name as my beloved first husband, Harry. Shortly after my Harry was killed in a hunting accident, this large gray and white cat showed up at the back door and scratched to be let in. When I opened it, he winked at me, walked in and made himself comfortable in Harry's recliner. I realize it's probably silly but I've always felt that my Harry sent him along to keep me company—or to convey his opinions which I could frequently live without.

"You know what she's like." I called after his swishing tail. Then just to be mean, I added, "Like a dog with a bone."

I heard grumbling from the living room. I smiled.

Gabe came in from his garage office to see what we had for dinner.

"You're still thinking about the cruise, aren't you?"

I shrugged.

"Why? Is it because you hate to miss out on something?"

My eyes widened in horror. "Are you comparing me to Dee?"

"Sweetheart, I am simply suggesting that you're making kind of a big deal out of this. So the guild is going and you don't want to go. Let them go."

"Dee wants to go."

He chuckled. "Of course she does. She'll get over it."

I looked at him dubiously. "Have you met her?"

He blew out a breath and nodded. "Okay, she'll never let you hear the end of it." Then he added, "Maybe Queenie would let her go without you."

I gave him another look of the same.

"Right, why would she do that? They all know what Diane's like." He took a breath and grinned. "AND she would still never let you forget it."

Later that night, we had dinner and played Jeopardy with Harry. Here's the thing: he takes his place in his recliner between our recliners, listens and watches, and says something in cat to every other answer. Yes, we cheer him on and pretend he's right and thank heaven no one is recording this.

I went to bed but lay awake, listening to Gabe's light snores, and thinking. Did I want to go with the girls? Was it about being left out? Oh Lord. I was clearly spending too much time with Dee.

Three

I love my job and I usually brighten up when I walk into the library. But, after spending Sunday convincing myself that I was an adult and, if I didn't want to go on the water, there was absolutely no reason that I should. Dee would be upset but, hey, there was no reason she and I couldn't take a girl's trip somewhere on dry land. I could turn this into a win-win.

Why, then, was this gray cloud over my head on Monday morning as I got my coffee in the breakroom? I went up to my office and started on the first of the week activities. Mondays were actually my busiest days since I typically took Saturday and Sunday off. I started clearing emails and opening mail.

Lucy, my assistant head librarian, came in clutching her cup of coffee. "Everything okay, Miranda?" She looked at me carefully.

"Fine." I replied firmly. "Why?"

She grinned. "Well, for one thing, you're shredding that mail like you mean it."

I managed a smile. "Sorry. Something's come up. You know, one of those things you don't want to do but for some reason think you should do although no one probably really cares if you don't do it."

She took a seat in front of my desk. "Wow. Would you care to translate that?"

So I told her about the cruise and how the other quilters were going and we always went to quilting things together and now Dee wanted to go.

"Oh boy, Diane wants to go?" Her smiled faded. She stood and cleared her throat. "Okay, good luck with that." She edged toward the door. "I'll be in my office then."

"Right."

I knew she wouldn't be gone for long. On Mondays she usually brought me up to speed on what had happened over the weekend while we ate lunch in my office.

Sure enough, the morning flew by and about noon, she poked her head in the door. "Any special requests?"

I gave it some thought. "How about pizza? We haven't had that for a while?"

"Okay with me. I'll call it in."

She was back in a few minutes and settled herself in front of my desk with her iPad.

I closed my laptop and gave her my attention. Even if only one person got upset or one idea came up over the weekend, I needed to know.

The pizza showed up in twenty minutes (benefits of a small town) and we went over to the small conference table to chow down.

We ate in contented silence for a bit, then Lucy cleared her throat.

"Yes?"

"I know it's none of my business…"

I waved her to continue.

"But I was thinking that maybe this issue with the cruise is kind of more about you overcoming something that you're afraid to do. I mean it's not like skydiving or cliff jumping or swimming with sharks or …"

Cliff jumping? Sharks? My food was starting to tumble in my stomach. "Okay, point taken. So what are you thinking?"

"Well, my Mom went to see a therapist to overcome, well never mind, but he was really nice and seemed to help. You do have a few weeks before the cruise. I have a feeling that you want to prove to yourself you can do it; it's not really about the other women. So maybe he could help you."

She looked at me with her big blue eyes and sincere freckled face.

The idea of taking steps to prepare was starting to sink in. "Thanks, Lucy."

She beamed and gave a little sigh of relief.

I couldn't wait to get home and tell Gabe. At five, I hurried out of the library.

I found him in the kitchen as he so often is these days. I don't mind that he's a better cook than I am. It's really nice to not have to think about dinner when I'm working.

"Hey there, gorgeous." He came forward in his adorable striped chef's apron to give me a hug. "How was your day, dear?" He said in a teasing and overly-polite tone.

"Cute. Actually, pretty good."

I waited until we were at the table and then I told him Lucy's take on the situation.

He put his fork down. "So let me see if I follow. You're going to see a therapist to overcome your fear so that you can go do something you don't want to do, have never wanted to do, and don't really need to do now."

"Geez, when you put it that way, it sounds stupid."

He gave me a snarky grin.

"I prefer to think of it as challenging myself to expand my horizons by venturing out of my comfort zone."

He shook his head. "I will never understand women."

I returned his snarky grin. "You got that right."

He took my hand across the table and squeezed it. "You shall remain a mysterious but lovely and beguiling creature to me."

One of the things I love about Gabe is his ability to make me laugh.

Four

On Tuesday morning, I was feeling a bit more chipper. I had gotten an appointment with Dr. Jonathon Locke for Thursday at 6PM. I thanked Lucy again for her referral and we moved forward to discuss matters not resolved yesterday.

Okay, I put off calling Myrtle Jeffers to tell her she could not have a copy of the book she asked for because it was on pre-order and wasn't printed yet. Myrtle did not take kindly to being told "no." We also once again had to call John Kane to remind him that he had to bring back his overdue books. John felt that, as a taxpayer, he could "keep them as long as I damn well please, thank you."

Lucy and I flipped for it and I won, i.e., I got to call Myrtle. She took the defeat gracefully and went to tackle John. This often involved running by his house.

Around eleven, my cell phone rang, an infrequent occurrence.

"Hey, Dee."

"Miranda, I was wondering if we could grab lunch."

"Geez, what's the occasion?"

She chuckled. "I have a three-hour break in the middle of the day."

"Good enough." I paused only a second. "Sylvia's at 1?"

"Can you make it 12:30?"

"Sure. See ya."

I looked forward to it. It had been a couple of weeks since I'd eaten at Sylvia's, although Gabe picked up our dinner there about once a week. Gabe may be a better cook than me but Sylvia's got us both beat by a mile.

I got there early and ordered us two iced teas. Sylvia's been jazzing things up a bit and today she was offering a "special": a chopped salad with chicken, bacon, avocado, and other yummy things served with a dipping sauce. I'd ask for the recipe but, being honest with myself, knew I'd never actually make it when I could swing by here and get one.

However, I waited politely for Diane before ordering.

She breezed in and threw her tote on the bench seat. "Did you order yet?"

"No, I waited for you."

She shot me a puzzled look. "Isn't today Tuesday—chopped salad special?"

I grinned and raised two fingers toward Sylvia who nodded.

"Okay then, we're all set."

Dee took a long swig of her tea and then said formally, "You're probably wondering why I asked you here."

I couldn't resist not playing along. "Not really. We have lunch together like once a week."

"Cute. However, there is a point I'd like to make." She took a breath. "You don't have to go on this cruise just for me. I need to respect your fears and let it go. So it's fine. We'll plan something else." It all came out in a rush and, before I could respond, Sylvia plopped the two salads and sauce cups in front of us.

"Anything else?" She eyed Dee suspiciously.

Dee gave her a lovely smile. "No thanks, honey. We'll pick up the complimentary antacids on our way out."

Sylvia stalked off.

Dee's smile turned to a wicked grin. I shook my head. She and Sylvia have been going at each other for years. No reason, they both enjoyed it as far as I could tell.

"You think those up ahead of time, don't you?"

"Absolutely. I have a notebook in case something occurs to me."

I still hadn't responded to Dee's offer to forego the cruise. I thought it over while we both dug into the delicious salads.

"What brought this on?" I finally asked.

She shrugged. "I told Mark about it and he said I was being selfish. He, uh, told me to say that stuff."

I nodded. I've always liked Mark. "Well, Lucy told me about a therapist who might be able to help me overcome my fear of, hmm, drowning. I have an appointment Thursday night."

She brightened. "Really? So you're willing to try?"

I half shrugged. "We'll see."

"Great." And she was off and running. "Because I was thinking you should go over to the Y and take a few swim lessons. Not to become an Olympic swimmer or anything but to become more comfortable in the water. I was talking to Ethan, he's on the swim team at Penn, you know, and the idea came to me. He won't be home for a couple of weeks but his friend Felix is a great guy and I'm sure he could teach you. What do you think?"

I stopped eating. "Back up here. Swim lessons, at my age?"

She frowned, shaking her brown curls. "What do you mean, at your age? And be very careful here because your age is my age." She waved a finger at me and pulled a piece of paper out of her bag. "Here's the number. He can get you in tomorrow at 5."

Five

The thought did occur to me that I maybe should have seen the therapist before I took the swim lessons but time was limited.

"I'm off to a swim lesson."

"Can I come?" Gabe said with a twinkle in his eye.

I held up my "stop" hand and he moved quickly out to his office in our garage where I could not hear him chuckling.

I hurried over to the Y and found the female changing room. I put on the bathing suit that I had dug out of the very bottom of my underwear drawer even though it seemed a bit smaller than I remembered, put on my swim cap with a snap, tightened my goggles and added my nose pinch thing. I looked like an alien in the mirrored wall as I entered the pool area. Why on earth would you put a mirrored wall there?

Two things struck me at once—the overwhelming smell of chlorine and the hot dampness of the air, closely followed by the squeals of happy kids. A six-year old kicked his way over to the edge of the pool.

"Is that you, Aunt Miranda? Come on in, it's fun." Jackson Bartlett yelled loud enough that I'm sure the woman at the front desk heard him.

I nodded and gave a little wave. I had paid for a private lesson, for heaven's sake. This kind of humiliation would be exactly the reason I had never taken lessons before.

Brittany's husband, John, appeared next to me.

"Hey, Miranda. I hear you girls are going on a cruise."

I nodded.

He shrugged. "I told Brit to go. She could use the break. I can handle the kids." At that moment, a splash of water smacked us both.

"Okay, you. That's it. Get out." He said as he sputtered.

Childish laughter ensued. But the boy did as instructed and padded his way over to us across the wet cement deck.

"Sorry, Dad. It was an accident."

"Sure." John ruffled the kid's hair. "Kid's hour is over, anyway, dude. Get your sister and let's head into the dressing room."

Jackson called and waved and his four-year-old sister swam over to the steps and hopped out.

"Aunt Miranda!" The little wet body slammed into me, sending water dripping down my legs. I patted her wet cap.

"Hey, Samantha. You guys are awesome." I mumbled.

"Now it's time for the grown-ups to swim." She pointed a small finger at me and then at the water. "That's you. Go ahead."

I took a breath and looked around. A tall thin college age guy stepped out of the dressing room door.

"Mrs. Downing?"

I nodded.

"I'm Felix." He grinned. "Okay, we're going to start with holding your breath underwater just to get you used to the idea of being in the water, okay?"

I gamely followed him down to the steps. The pool was now, thankfully, almost empty. A few adults started swimming laps at the far side.

After I had dunked under and held my breath several times, he asked me if there was any special reason I was taking lessons, you know, now. I ignored the implication that I had waited until near death.

"I'm going on a cruise and I'm nervous about, well, the water."

His eyes narrowed and a frown wrinkle appeared. "You mean, you think that taking swim lessons will help you, uh, not worry about…"

"Yeah, drowning."

He chuckled. "Mrs. Downing. No worries. If you fall off a cruise ship, you'll be dead when you hit that water. It would be like hitting concrete after falling off a hundred foot building, you get that, right?"

I swallowed hard. I'm an idiot but there was no need for further humiliation. "Of course I know that. I just want to spend a little time around water."

He relaxed. "Great, okay. Next I'll teach you how to back float. See, you can float for hours, very little effort. So if you go to a pool party or something, you'll be all set."

Laying on my back with his arm under me, it took a few tries but I got it finally. He gave me a big thumbs up as I clambered out of the pool.

He wasn't fooling me. I could hear his nasty little mental wheels spinning how he was going to tell his friends about the old lady who thought she could learn to swim in two or three easy lessons and then survive either falling off a cruise ship or a sinking one.

"See you Wednesday!" He said cheerfully and dove back into the pool, taking long strokes with his young long arms. I kind of hated that kid.

For my next lesson, I lost the nose clip thing and the goggles so I didn't stand out so much. I marched boldly to the steps and walked into the water, acclimating to the chill while I waited for Felix.

"Hey, look at you!" He said in that fake cheerful condescending voice.

I smiled back. "So what are we up to today?"

"I thought we'd try diving to the bottom of the pool to pick up a quarter. It's like a pool game everyone plays."

I stared at him.

He punched me lightly in the arm. "Just kidding. You really need to lighten up."

You have no idea how badly I wanted to punch him back.

Six

I was almost as nervous about seeing the therapist as I was about the swim lessons. What if this person hypnotized me into thinking I was a chicken or something? I'd seen those shows. What if he convinced me to kill someone or rob a bank? I'd seen that on TV, too. Or, dear Lord, what if he accidentally brainwashed me into thinking I was an Olympic swimmer? I could dive without a care into the ship pool and, you know, drown.

I was the only patient in the waiting room and that suited me fine. I thumbed through a magazine from 2015 and noted how much older some movie stars had gotten in the last five years.

Finally, the inner door opened. Dr. Locke was a Judd Hirsch lookalike with a kind, trustworthy face, curly gray hair with a little bald spot, of a suitable age. I wondered if he would consider giving swim lessons on the side.

After the introductions, he asked why I was there.

"Oh, well, you see, I have a chance to go on a cruise, a quilting cruise with the guild that I belong to. I guess I don't like the idea that my fear of water is holding me back."

He nodded. "Is it a fear of water or a fear of drowning?"

Suddenly I knew we were going to get along fine. "Drowning."

"Seems reasonable to me. But I understand why you don't want it to keep you from joining your friends." He paused a second. "Now, before we begin, is there anything about coming to see me that makes you nervous or upset?"

I told him I was concerned about being hypnotized. He stared at me for a second and then gave me a big smile.

"That's not what I do, Mrs. Downing. Relax. I'm just going to make a few suggestions to help you get control of your fear. It's called desensitization therapy."

"Okay." I hesitated. "You can call me Miranda."

"Fine, thank you, and you can call me David. Now, is there any other step you're taking to get over your fear?"

I nodded proudly. "I'm taking swim lessons."

"Well, that's an excellent start," he said encouragingly, "but it's not very relaxing, is it?"

"Oh dear, no."

"Right. So here's something else I'd like you to try that is a little easier. I'd like you to spend some time in a hot tub, preferably with some soothing music nearby."

Boy, that sounded good. The Day Spa has a gorgeous hot tub; I had a gift card once. "I can do that."

He smiled. "You look like you're ready to go right now."

I sighed. "It sounds so relaxing."

"That's the idea."

As you might expect, he asked about any water-related incidents in my childhood that I don't think it's necessary to go into here. I have to admit, it did give me a better understanding of where my water phobia came from.

Before I knew it, a little timer dinged and the doctor stood.

"It was lovely to meet you, Miranda. I think it would be good if you came back next week. I don't want you to think this is a life-long commitment but let's have one more go, if that's all right."

"I can do that."

"I'd like to give you one bit of homework."

I was all ears. I've always loved homework. I'm the one.

"I want you to research cruise ships, especially the one you'll be travelling on."

The confused look on my face let him know I required more information. I hadn't planned on driving the ship or writing a travel guide about it.

"It's simple, Miranda. The more information you have, the less fear there will be. For example, if you found out that the ship has been running this route for five years, eight times a year, and never had a problem, wouldn't you feel better?"

"Absolutely."

"That's the point. I can tell you that, as soon as you board the ship, there will be a mandatory safety drill. Every passenger is assigned to a life boat station and told what to do in the event of an emergency. So you see, the staff on cruise lines are well trained and there is a system just in case."

I let out a long breath. "Good to know."

He stood. "Okay, now come back next Thursday same time and let me know how you're doing." He came around the desk and walked me to the door.

"I can tell you're a strong person, Miranda. You're going to be fine. With a bit of work, you might even be able to enjoy yourself on this cruise."

"Thank you, David."

What a relief! I loved this guy.

Seven

"You will be careful, won't you?" My husband was frowning as he gave me a final hug.

"Don't worry. I'll look after her." Dee bounced up and down, energy flying off her. "This is so exciting!"

Gabe looked at her, then back at me, the frown a little deeper. I smiled at him to let him know I got the message.

"We'll be fine, darling. Enjoy the peace and quiet."

"Not sure I'll get much of that. I have a feeling Harry's going to be a nightmare."

Our cat Harry had made his feelings known about me leaving by giving me an earful of annoyed cat grumbles and then stalking off without saying goodbye.

"He'll settle down once he realizes I've gone despite his disapproval. I'll call or text when I can."

Some small part of me hated to see him drive away. Some slightly larger part of me wanted to run after the car and jump in.

Diane gripped my arm firmly. "Don't even think about it. I'm so glad you're coming. I've never been on a cruise before!"

I took a breath. "Me neither." And there was a reason for that.

We checked our bags, got our boarding passes and moved along to the gate. The other guild members were there and it felt good to be with our group.

Queenie and Sarah, our now experienced cruisers, knew what they were doing so they shepherded the rest of us--Dee, Judy, Shelby, and me--through the next few hours of travel like tour guides.

We boarded the plane and settled in for the flight. It was only three hours so that was not so bad. I had several books on my Kindle and a bit of hand sewing although, looking around at my fellow guild members, I could have borrowed anything from a paperback to a quilt-as-you-go square to a Sudoku puzzle book with no problem. Overall, I find that quilters simply don't waste time. Idle hands and all that.

We landed in Fort Lauderdale, met up at the luggage carousel, and waited for everyone to find their bags before moving toward the shuttle pick-up. The ship had several land stops and a Captain's Dinner which required nicer dress so not one of us thought we could pull it off with just a carryon.

Queenie and Sarah in the lead, we moved to the outdoor pick up spot and the shuttle, brightly emblazoned with "Caribbean Voyager" pulled up shortly. Luggage stowed, we settled in for the short ride to the port. I calmed myself by repeating the details of the ship in my head, as Dr. Locke had recommended.

And there it was! If you've never seen a cruise ship before, it is *big*. I'm talking jaw-dropping big as in equivalent to a high-rise building big. I stopped cold and I'm pretty sure my jaw dropped like a country girl coming to the big city for the first time.

Dee kept me moving as we went through check-in much like that at the airport—luggage tags, security scans, and all. We were issued key cards that would serve as room keys and charge cards on board the ship. Moving up the gangplank was an out-of-body experience.

A super cheerful crew member checked our new cards and directed us to a lounge which had lovely snack tables waiting. There were cute little sandwiches, bags of cookies and chips, and bottled drinks. I finally took a breath. This was simply the first time, and it certainly would not be the last, that I would realize the cruise company knew what it was doing. Most of their new arrivals (like us) had probably spent the day getting there with little time for food along the way. We helped ourselves and then went outside to watch the rest of the passengers board.

Have you ever noticed that at any departure, there's always that one couple that arrives last minute and seems to be running for it? We watched as a short, chubby woman with white hair and a tall bald man bolted along the walkway and zipped up the gangplank. The crew member holding the gate open for them gave them a big smile as she waved them through. When they made it, a small smattering of applause went up. The lady gave a big wave and the man took a bow.

Then the whistle blew to announce the ship's departure.

I took a couple of deep breaths and the food I had just eaten rumbled uneasily.

"Come on, Miranda. Let's find our room!" Dee took my arm and pulled me inside. Following the maps we'd been given, we went into the central atrium area and down the steps.

"Here we are." She stopped outside #618. "Hey, look at that." She pointed to our luggage which was stacked beside the door.

"That's impressive." I gave her a smile. I knew that Dee was going to do her best to make this cruise comfortable for me. Even though I also knew that was partly out of guilt since she had talked me into coming, I still thought it was sweet.

My reading had prepared me to be squeezed into a closet so I was pleasantly surprised to find that I was in a decent-sized room with two twin beds, a dresser, desk, and a closet. Everything was built in and every inch of space used. The term "stowed away" came to mind. I knew that everything o a boat was stowed away so it wouldn't fly around in a storm. I decided not to dwell on that.

I checked out the bathroom which was, to be polite, compact and meant for thinner people. I could put my hand on the shower wall and touch the mirror above the sink.

Diane stuck her head in and quickly ducked back out. "Like, whoa," she muttered.

On the desk, there were two plastic bags full of paperwork with our names on them. In addition to the daily schedule for quilting presentations, there was a list of excursions we could go on as extras to which I gave short shrift; I doubted I'd be scuba diving or jet skiing or any of the other mostly water-required activities.

There was a postcard inviting us to choose the 6PM dinner seating or the 8PM for the rest of the cruise and requesting that we bring the cards to tonight's buffet dinner and put them in the collection box. We grinned at each other and marked the earlier time. We run on small town time and would never last until the 8PM setting.

Not that we would want for food, I had counted 10 restaurants on board in addition to the dining room. That certainly explained why so many people who have been on a cruise ship talk about the food more than most everything else! It appeared to be available 24/7 from midnight buffet in the atrium area to the Early Risers breakfast bar that opened at 4AM to the self-serve kiosks that would hold you over during that gap.

We unpacked what we could and then my phone announced a text from Queenie. "All meet at Grandview Buffet hall in 15 minutes."

Eight

"Okay, three decks up, hang a right, across the atrium, it's right there." Dee studied the map that came with our papers.

"Or," I waved a hand, "we can follow the crowd."

Once we entered the dining hall, we spotted Shelby, our youngest member, guarding a round table for six. She waved us to go ahead and we joined the moving queue.

Without causing unnecessary drooling, let me simply say that the buffet was probably at least forty feet long, divided into salads, fruit plates, carving stations, vegetables, desserts, breads and rolls. As I said, I wasn't starving but it wouldn't hurt to sample small bits of things, would it? Plates loaded, we scooted into the bench seats and Shelby took off to join the line.

There were glass doors at the end of the hall and I could see the wake the ship was creating as it moved. I quickly looked away and focused on my food. Everyone was excited to be on board and looking forward to the after-dinner welcome speech one of the quilt instructors was giving.

After sampling for an hour or so, we walked out into the atrium and found our way to the large theater lounge which was filled with row after row of seats. It was about half full of laughing, talking folks, mostly women but with a few men as well. Quilting has long since become an equal opportunity art.

"Dear Lord, this place is massive!" I heard Judy exclaim behind me. Judy, another cruising rookie, is the mother of a college-aged son and had gotten us started on our adventures with her inherited quilted skirt that held hidden jewels. She's a lovely woman and I'm not just saying that because she gave me a Victorian settee! It occurred to me as I turned toward her that this might be her first time out of Pennsylvania.

"960 people max capacity," I confirmed automatically.

Her eyes widened and then she laughed out loud. I heard other chuckles as well.

Shelby took the ball and ran with it. "Hey Miranda, how many passengers does the ship hold?

"2103."

"How long is it?"

"1002 feet."

"How many crew?"

"910."

"Okay, that's enough. Stop tormenting Miranda." Queenie shook her head and waved a red-tipped hand toward the front where our speaker had appeared. "Let the woman speak."

The speaker turned out to be a pixie like our missing Quilt Guild member Brittany (who had stayed home with her baby), petite and fit looking but with blonde hair where Brit's is brown.

"Good evening, fellow quilters and welcome to the Voyager."

"Good evening." We all said back in unison like school children. An embarrassed chuckle followed as we realized we had done that.

"I'm Laurie Lambert, one of the quilt instructors on board. I'm sure you've all had a long day already. So I'm going to give you a quick overview and let you begin to enjoy your time onboard.

"There are four of us on board rotating through the demonstrations which are dictated by the ship's travel schedule. So you will note that there are only two demos tomorrow since many of you will be ashore in Key West. On the days we are cruising all day, there will be four demos. You have a full schedule in your rooms. If you don't, see me and I'll give you one." She smiled as she waved the paper.

"Finally, there will be an old-fashioned quilting bee later in the week and a gathering where you can chat with other quilters. We hope that you pick up some tips, have some fun, and enjoy each other's company." She held up a clipboard. "We do ask that you sign up for the quilting bee as space is limited for that one."

Lots of nods. "For the other demos, there are lots of seats available so please don't worry about signing up, just come on in when you can. Feel free to stop me if you see me around the ship and you have any questions. Thank you for coming. Good night."

Some of the quilters gathered around her but I was happy to slip away and I noticed the other members of our Cutler crew left, too. Travel is fun but getting there, especially through airports, is more tiring than fun.

As we headed out, an announcement blared out that it was time for the safety drill. Dee looked at me and I directed her to our appointed location. Several crew members went through the location of the lifeboats we should head for, showed us the boxes along the deck in which the life vests were stored, etc.

Other passengers nearby seemed to be whispering among themselves or wandering away, attention-wise, but I listened intently, taking notes on my phone. Yes, I saw Dee edging away from me but better embarrassed than water-logged, I say.

Dee was still wound up and wanted to wander around the ship but I opted to find my back to the room. I had already realized I should enjoy any quiet moment I could get. I sent Gabe a quick text letting him know that I had survived the first day. I read in peace until Dee burst in.

"Oh, Miranda! This ship is so awesome." She threw herself down on her bed. I put my book down and listened to her adventure. The woman knew how to cover ground. She had been to the casino, the gift shop, the ice cream stand, and back to the theater lounge to listen to some music from the live band on board.

As soon as it looked like she was done, I quickly went into the bathroom and put on my pajamas. She took the hint and did the same, then quieted down. I fell asleep faster than I expected near midnight.

Since we had an inside cabin with no windows, it really was easy to pretend I was in a hotel room, safe on land.

Nine

Cruise Day 2 (Key West)

Next thing I knew, it was morning, at least it felt like morning. Without a window, the light in the room hadn't changed. But my phone screen read 7:30 which is my usual wake time at home and that was a relief. Getting a good night's rest on board alleviated one of my concerns. I got up and dressed as quietly as I could but when I came out of the bathroom, Dee was yawning and stretching.

"Wait for me." She jumped up and grabbed clothes out of her drawer.

Okay, maybe I had been trying to let her sleep or maybe I was going to sneak off to breakfast without her. But I did realize that while I was at quilting events, she'd be on her own so I settled down on the edge of the bed to wait for her. We chatted our way to the breakfast buffet and found Sarah and Queenie at the same table as yesterday, now officially the Cutler Quilt Guild #1 table.

Shelby and Judy were still asleep. Sarah said they were going to give them another half hour and then ring the rooms so they would have time for a bite before we docked at Key West around 9AM. She grinned and said maybe Judy didn't realize what she was in for keeping up with Shelby.

The window wall still showed a lot of water out there but I convinced myself that we were going to land soon so it was nothing to worry about. Surely, the lifeboats could make it that far. Besides, I could back float if I had to.

"The quilt demos for today look pretty entry level so I'd rather see Key West. Are you two heading on shore?" Queenie asked.

Dee and I looked at each other.

"Absolutely."

"Sure."

I'd heard a lot of wonderful things about Key West. Besides, was I going to miss an opportunity to spend time on dry land? I don't think so.

Sarah said, "You know, I've actually been there before. I think I'll stay on board and get a feel for where things are, relax on the deck, that sort of thing." She smiled, "I've got some hand quilting with me."

Shelby and Judy came in, threw us a wave, and went straight for the buffet.

When they settled in to nosh, Shelby was full of stories of how they watched the moon over the water. Judy managed a smile but looked more tired than enthusiastic.

"We're all going into Key West except Sarah." Queenie told her. "What would you two like to do today?"

"If it's okay, I'd like to stay on board and see if there are some kids, uh, my age and maybe hang around the pool." She looked at Sarah for approval.

"It's okay, honey, we all realize we're not kids anymore. I'm sure you'll be fine onboard. Besides, I'm staying on the ship myself. Check in with me later."

"Excellent." Shelby beamed.

"No way I'm missing Key West." Judy drank her coffee down in one gulp and went back for seconds.

We all knew that four people in a group made for awkward going. So Judy and Queenie opted to explore as a pair and Dee and I decided to go our own way.

"Now, if you like, we could meet at Beaches Café. I did a little research last night and it really looks lovely." Queenie suggested.

"Sounds good."

I'm not gonna lie; I was very happy when my feet hit the ground. The ship was actually able to dock right at the edge of Key West so when we came down the gangplank, there were stands of taxis and scooter rentals right in front of us.

We waved our goodbyes to Queenie and Judy and passed by the transportation area, walking up the street instead. There were some brightly-colored houses that we could see close by. We strolled around the block, getting our land legs and admiring the architecture.

I spotted a beach across the street dotted with palm trees. We made our way over and stood there, watching the water and the sun sparkle. We were warm and content for about ten minutes before Dee started to twitch to move on.

Our time was limited so we made our way to one of the must-sees as noted in the single-page brochure the ship had included for us, Ernest Hemingway's house. As we approached, Queenie and Judy waved at us from the line. We all laughed and then Dee and I got our tickets and joined the back of the line. The house was lovely, the garden was magnificent, the swimming pool was really big, and the famous six-toed cats did indeed look like they were wearing mittens.

We checked our time and found we could make a quick run at the Harry Truman Little White House before lunch. We share a love of looking at other people's houses. This 1890 home served pretty much as Truman's Camp David. It was lovely and full of presidential memorabilia as other presidents spent time here too. It was easy to see how relaxing it would be after life in Washington.

We hurried down to the restaurant. Queenie and Judy were already drinking something pretty out of tall glasses. We all went with the conch fritters on the open-air deck facing the water, feeling warm and comfortable here by now. There is a relaxed happy feeling in places like this that makes for a special experience. If someone could bottle the calm, they'd make a fortune!

Dee and I meandered into a couple of shops, including Margaritaville as a tribute to Jimmy Buffet and The Kitty Shop where I looked at several sweaters for Harry. Then I had an image of me trying to get one on him and decided maybe not such a good idea. I settled for a small bag of treats. Most of the shops showed little rainbows if not flags indicating that the gay community was welcome and active here as well. For some reason, that touched my heart. This lovely sunny place had no room in it for hate and that seemed right to me.

We moved on and were not surprised when the four of us met up again at the Mel Fisher Treasure Museum.

I thought I caught a glimpse of Laurie, the woman who had welcomed us last night, with a tall dark-haired man on the street. The couple stood out among the happy, laughing crowd by the sour looks on their faces. He looked annoyed and she looked like she really wanted to be somewhere else. I also noticed the grip he had on her arm, as if he thought she was going to run away. I pulled my attention back to what Dee was saying and decided to put it out of my mind. While it seemed a shame not to be enjoying this gorgeous, sunny place, not everybody is happy all the time.

By 4:00, Dee and I were ready to go back to the ship, with souvenirs to show for our visit and healthy pink faces.

As we waited in line at security at the bottom of the gangplank, I saw another somewhat familiar face. It took me a moment to place her.

"Virginia Hamilton?" I said half to myself and half out loud.

She turned and smiled. "Hi, have we met?"

I turned a little pinker. "Not really. I attended your session at the Lancaster Pennsylvania Quilt Show."

Her smile faded a little around the edges. "Ah, and you are?"

"Miranda Downing."

Her eyes widened just enough for me to realize she knew something of my involvement with the solving of

Eleanor Jones' murder which was tied to that quilt show. Unfortunately, Mrs. Jones' popularity as "The Quilting Queen" meant that her death made more than national headlines and my name did too.

"Of course. Nice to see you."

As soon as we got up and onto the ship, Virginia moved away, fast.

Dee giggled. "I think she remembers you."

I had to smile myself. "I think you're right."

We dumped our goodies in our room and showered and changed for dinner which did call for some interesting choreography. This wasn't the formal Captain's Dinner but we thought it warranted sundresses with a light sweater rather than shorts and shirts.

I wasn't surprised to find that we were seated with six fellow passengers we had never met. I read that the cruise lines do this in an effort to get their cruisers to meet new people. In our case, it worked out well (so I could chalk another worry off my list).

Two were fellow quilters and I chatted cheerfully with them and their spouses. The other couple was schoolteachers who had decided last minute to grab a cruise and this happened to be the one they got (free to them with some points system). Apparently, they loved cruising and did it several times a year. Dee was enthralled with all the places they had been and they were delighted to talk to her about them clear through dessert and coffee.

After dinner, we were free to roam and somehow gravitated toward the casino. Sipping our complimentary cocktails and playing slots, I would never tell Dee but I was totally unaware of my fear of water at that moment and actually relaxed.

I noticed that Laurie and that dark-haired man were in the high stakes slot area. Now I felt pretty sure he was her husband just by the vibes they were giving off. I squinted to read the sign by the door. *$500 min.* Holy Toledo, she sure wasn't making that kind of money as a quilt instructor! She didn't look any happier now than she had earlier. Maybe her husband has a gambling problem. Note to self: not my problem.

I pulled myself back to my machine.

"What's up?" Dee whispered from the machine next to me. "I just won $20 and you weren't even watching."

"Laurie's over there with a dark-haired man I saw her with earlier on Key West."

"Where?"

"The high stakes slot area."

Dee gasped. "Get out."

"Geez louise, don't stare."

She stared in that direction until Laurie noticed.

"For heaven's sake, Dee, stop staring." I hissed.

Laurie murmured something in the man's ear and then came our way.

"'Evening, ladies."

"Hello," we said in unison.

She laughed. "You're quilters, right?"

"I am, she's not." I said quickly. "Dee's just along for the cruise."

Laurie nodded. "Excellent. Well, I'll see you tomorrow then. My first demo is applique at 10AM if you're interested." She addressed that to me, her eyes meeting mine in a way that made me feel uncomfortable.

"I haven't honestly read through tomorrow's schedule yet," I muttered, looking down.

"No worries. Hope you're having a good time." She walked away and went straight out the doors to the deck.

Dee and I both automatically looked back to the guy she had left behind. He sent a frozen glare our way. I know this because I took a shiver and I heard Dee swallow. We left our seats and moved to another area of the casino out of his view.

We played another half hour and then went in search of a snack before bed. Dee, of course, knew exactly where to go and we both scored hot fudge sundaes which we spooned into on our way back to our room.

I finished mine while I looked at the schedule. Since we were going to be on the water all day tomorrow (something I did not need to dwell on), there were four sessions of an hour each.

Laurie's applique was first at 10; Virginia was on at 12:30 and she was doing redwork which had always intrigued me, a woman we hadn't met named Allison Hopewell was doing embroidery embellishments at 3, and Jennifer Myers was on at 5:00 with hand quilting without a frame.

Dee's daily schedule was, of course, a bit different. Hers had aquacize in the pool at 8, bingo at 10, trivia at 12 in the lounge, jazzercise at 2:30, and options for a load of fun stuff that made me want to rethink my own priorities.

Ultimately, we decided we'd both do bingo at 10, then I'd go to the 12:30 quilt demo while Dee played trivia and walked the deck. We agreed to meet for lunch at the pizza parlor at 1:30 or whenever I could get there after my demo. I really wanted to go to the 5:00 session so that left us free to plan the afternoon after the pizza (which likely included a nap—at least for me).

Pleased with ourselves for being so decisive, we read for a while and turned in. Just as we were turning out the light, we heard voices outside our door. If they had been low and quiet, we wouldn't even have noticed. But they weren't.

"Laurie, what is wrong with you?" A male voice asked.

"I don't want to do this anymore. You're gonna get caught." A woman replied.

"I think you mean, we're gonna get caught, right?"He lowered his voice. "This is the best gig I've ever had and don't you even think about screwing it up, you hear me?"

"Ow." The female voice gasped in pain.

I sat straight up. Dee did the same and we looked at each other in the dim light of the bathroom nightlight.

"You heard that?" she said.

I nodded, then realized she might not be able to see me. "Yeah, sure did."

"You know, "she started. "Yep." I finished. "If you were going to put a voice to the guy in the casino…"

"That would be it."

Ten

Cruise Day 3 (Nothing but water)

I fell asleep determined to avoid that guy for the rest of the cruise. Dee's intentions were different as I found out the next morning.

"Listen," she said waving her toothbrush in my direction. "We have to find out what's going on with that guy. You know he's up to no good."

"No, we don't." I replied firmly. "What we need to do is get dressed and have a lovely leisurely breakfast, take a look at that shop that has the cool t-shirts, and meander down to bingo at 10."

Her chin rose, she got that "I'm not going to argue; I'll just do what I want anyway" look and said, "Sounds good."

To break up our buffet breakfast routine, we went to the French bistro (Chez Jean) for chocolate croissants. Then we did indeed meander around the interior of the ship pretending that we were walking off the croissants.

Bingo was fun, especially since neither of us had played in years and trying to play six cards was a challenge. I won a $25 card for the gift shop! There's no better feeling than throwing your arm up and yelling, "BINGO!"

When it was finished, Dee went off to play trivia and I went to my first quilting demo.

Despite our awkward encounter yesterday, I knew that Virginia Hamilton was a talented quilter and a charming speaker. So I looked forward to her presentation on redwork. It has always intrigued me but I've never done it. It's certainly different from piecing and quilting.

Essentially, it's a matter of embroidering on a white or neutral background with red thread. Sounds simple enough but you can take it to a lot of levels. We had a full-sized redwork medallion quilt at our quilt show. I was more likely to start with a pillow.

As I expected, Virginia started with a bit of the history (mid-19th century because red thread was the easiest color to obtain) and then showed us different sizes and types of pieces (from the delicate to the bold using yarn!). I guess the attraction for me was the portability of it: fabric, thread, needle and off you go. Also, you didn't have to worry about changing colors as you do with other embroidery.

It was new to me that redwork was now also being done in other single colors like black, blue, or green. When she finished up with a baby suit embroidered with a giraffe in black and the baby's name underneath, I was in. Have I mentioned my new grandson?

I was heading for the exit when one of the staff caught up to me.

"Mrs. Downing?"

"Yes?"

"Could you wait a minute? Ms. Hamilton would like to speak with you?"

I was surprised, to say the least. I was also hungry. "Okay."

I settled into a seat at the back of the room and waited until Virginia made her way to me. She sat down and smiled sheepishly.

"I first want to apologize for being so short with you yesterday. Seeing you and hearing your name brought back a lot of…painful memories. I still miss Eleanor every day."

"It's okay. I understand." And I did. Eleanor was the face of quilting. Her big smile was on TV, the internet, how-to videos, and lots of books. She had a way of taking the intimidation factor out of gorgeous intricate projects. She always said, "If I can do it, you can do it." We all believed her. There was simply no one else in line to fill her space in our lives. Watching her shows was a guilty pleasure of my own. It was sometimes hard to believe she was gone.

"No, it's not but you're kind to say so. And I also apologize for being so cloak and dagger, Mrs. Downing." Even as she said it, her eyes were roaming the area.

"Please call me Miranda."

"Thank you, and you can call me Ginny."

I nodded and waited. One thing I have learned from my husband is the advantage to waiting for the other person to speak what's on his or her mind.

She cleared her throat. "I'm actually speaking to you on Laurie's behalf." She hesitated, then continued, "she thinks you don't like her."

What? My mouth opened and I shut it. "I don't know her well enough to like or dislike her," I said briskly.

She laid a hand on my arm. "I'm sorry. I'm getting off to a bad start here. I told her I wasn't the person to approach you. Let me try again. Laurie knows, we both do, that you were involved in solving Eleanor's murder."

I wouldn't personally have put it that way since I was actually ambushed by her killer, having no idea she had done it, but I really wanted the woman to get on with it so I could go meet Dee for lunch. I settled for a nod and a shrug.

"Right." She lowered her voice. "Laurie has a problem and she's really scared. She doesn't know what to do about it. She is even afraid to be seen talking to you."

"Wow. That must be some problem."

She nodded. "She said you saw her in the casino with her husband, Mike."

"Only briefly."

She looked around at the empty room. "He's gotten in with some really bad people and they have him doing bad things that can only end up with him being dead or in prison." She took a breath. "Laurie is being drawn in with him and she just wants out, she wants it to stop."

"Define bad things."

She swallowed. "Well, I really don't want to go into that here." She looked around nervously.

This time, I took a breath. "And what on earth does she want me to do?"

Ginny blinked. "Well, she was, we were, hoping you could do something." She paused. "Isn't your husband an FBI agent?"

This time I blinked. "My husband's an ex-FBI agent and he only does private work now." I sighed. "You're really making it impossible for me to gauge the situation by not giving me any more information. I'm not a detective."

She patted my hand. "Of course not."

"Laurie really needs to reach out to law enforcement for help. They're not the bad guys, you know."

A look of horror crossed her face. "You don't understand. The people that are involved here have their own contacts in law enforcement. If she went to them, these people would find out. Mike and Laurie would both probably disappear without a trace soon after."

My brain was starting to absorb the size of her problem. "How long have you known Laurie?"

She looked surprised at the question. "I'd say about ten years."

I watched her face. "Do you believe her?"

She hesitated for only a fraction of a second. "Yes."

"Why?"

Her shoulders relaxed. "She's never lied to me, not once. And she seems so upset. Why would anybody make up something like this?"

She put her hand out. "Give me your phone and I'll put in my number in case you need to contact me."

I did what she asked; I was too busy thinking to pay attention. She handed it back to me and I took it automatically.

Why would anyone make this up? Well, that was the million dollar question, wasn't it? My first thought was to get rid of a husband they no longer wanted. It did seem a little extreme instead of divorce. To put the blame on the husband for something you were doing? Now there's a thought. But then I remembered the female voice outside my room, saying she didn't want to do this anymore.

It saddened me a little to realize that my experiences over the past several years had brought me to this cynical place. Five years ago, I believed everything that was said to me. Growing up in a small town had cocooned me in a soft blanket of complete safety and trust for a long time. But that had changed; I had changed.

"I hate to be rude to another quilter, Ginny, but I don't think I'm the person to help you."

She looked like she was going to burst into tears. "I knew I'd mess this up. Please wait." She frantically pushed numbers on her phone.

"It's me. You have to talk to her. Yes, now!" She handed me the phone.

"Mrs. Downing? It's Laurie Lambert."

"Hello," I said coolly.

"I'm so sorry. I had no right…" Her voice turned into a sob. "Just forget it, okay?" She clicked off.

Well, that was not what I expected. I looked at Ginny.

"What did she say?"

I swallowed, feeling guilty for no obvious reason. "She said to forget it."

"Oh." I swear her eyes filled with tears. She nodded and stood. "Okay then."

She hurried away.

I sat there for a few minutes. Forget it? How was I supposed to do that?

Harry was right. Coming on this cruise was a bad idea.

Eleven

I hurried down to meet Dee and found her at a table in the pizza parlor with a whole pizza and two iced teas in front of her. She sighed exaggeratedly and looked at her watch as I sat down.

"I got held up, hon. Sorry." I muttered.

"What's wrong?" Her eyes narrowed. "You look all…flustered."

I looked around and she did the same. "I'll tell you later."

"Okay but I have to hurry. I have jazzercise in about half an hour."

My eyes widened. "You're really doing that?"

She chuckled. "Have you seen the instructor?"

"Ah." I focused on my food. By the way, the food on this ship is everything you've heard and more. I'd have to start doing laps around the deck if I didn't want to go home five pounds heavier.

We finished up fast and went into a small lounge nearby that was not being used. I told Dee about the odd conversation I had with Ginny and the even odder one with Laurie.

She nodded. "I think maybe I know at least part of what's going on here."

I stared at her. "What?

Her face flushed a bit. "I followed him. He went straight to the casino as soon as it opened."

"I thought we agreed…"

Her chin rose in that all too familiar way. "I agreed to nothing."

"Right. He went straight to the casino."

She nodded eagerly. "And I'll bet he's still there."

I was confused. "So he has a gambling problem."

"I don't think so." She leaned toward me. "He's playing high stakes slots. He had a pile of those cash out tickets in front of him, too."

I waited, trying to hear what was interesting about this.

"Geez, Miranda, don't you ever watch Hawaii 5-0?" Her voice sank to a whisper. "Money laundering. That's how drug dealers do it. They swap out their drug money by putting money in the machines. They lose a little or win a little and then get a printout ticket they can cash in for clean money. Get it?"

"Not quite. So Mike Lambert…"

She interrupted impatiently. "Came on this cruise with his wife to launder money. We're in international waters so there's practically no law enforcement. And who's going to even notice?"

The light bulb came on. "Oh, Lord. If you think about it, what could be more inconspicuous than a boat half full of quilters? Wow, think of how many times they could get away with this if Laurie signs up as an instructor on different cruises?"

We looked at each other.

"I have to go." She pulled a couple of dance steps and a twirl. Dee's a wonderful person and a first-class English teacher but she'll never be on Dancing Stars, if you see what I mean.

"Don't do that." I threw her a finger pointing warning. I tickled myself with the idea of following her and taking pictures to post online but decided the chuckle that the idea gave me was enough.

It was coming up on 2 and my quilt demo was at 5 so I decided some reading and a nap might be in order. Still, I found myself at the casino and slipped inside. I put a $10 into the first machine I saw and started looking around.

Sure enough, Lambert was the only player in the high stakes area. I moved to a machine closer to where he was sitting, trying not to attract attention. Another couple conveniently parked themselves at machines across the aisle from him and distracted him.

I walked past and saw the pile of slips in front of him and, for the briefest of moments, he looked straight at me. Then he smiled and nodded. I made a beeline for the door.

I needed to clear my head so I made a lap around the deck, carefully keeping my eyes to the interior walls and staying at least ten feet from the rail. No problem.

I was making my final turn when I came face to face with Laurie. I faked a smile and slowed down. She seemed as startled as I was. She forced a return smile and nodded.

I leaned toward her. "I'll do what I can. No promises."

Her eyes lightened with tears. She nodded and whispered a 'thank you.'

I pulled my phone out and handed it to her down low. She quickly entered her number and pushed it back to me.

I raised my voice as two women passed us. "I really enjoyed your demonstration. Thanks for clearing that up." Then we quickly went our separate ways.

It felt like an undercover op. Dee would have loved it.

As I turned back toward my room, a dark shadow appeared in front of me.

"Mrs. Downing, isn't it?"

I caught my breath. "Yes. Have we met?"

"Not formally. Mike Lambert."

"Oh, Laurie's husband, of course. I think I saw you with her in the casino."

He smiled. "Right." He lowered his voice. "If we're going to be running into each other, I thought you should know that I know who you are."

He was almost a foot taller than me but I raised myself up to my full height. "And now I know who you are, too."
I brushed past him and didn't collapse until I got into our room.

Twelve

I took a cool shower to calm myself down. I tried to read my book but couldn't concentrate, reading the same page over and over. Finally, I lay down on my bed and simply closed my eyes, thought calm thoughts, and waited until time to dress for dinner since I was going directly there after the demo.

When I entered the big lounge, several hands went up in the air and waved. I shouldn't have been surprised that Queenie, Sarah, and Judy were attending this one. Shelby was off with some girls she'd met on board.

Jennifer Myers was tall and enviably thin with bright red hair pulled into a ponytail and an infectious grin.

"Good afternoon. I hope I can make hand quilting a little more relaxing and less difficult for those of you who haven't mastered using a hoop or frame. It is not a heresy to do without. In fact," her face fell a teeny bit, "our beloved Eleanor Jones loved to quilt without a hoop. Yes, there is a video. It seems that something as simple as this didn't get as much press as her more dramatic projects."

We sat fascinated as she talked us through layering and pinning without a frame, using fingerless gloves to ease the pain in the wrist and fingers, marking only small areas at a time so it wouldn't smudge off, and all kinds of great tips. She even gave us permission not to use a thimble!

She told us this remarkable story of passing through a small town in Kentucky and spotting a church quilting event. One woman there hung her layers on the wall and quilted up and down! She said if she hadn't seen it, she wouldn't have believed it. Then, as a finale, she picked up a quilt block and, fingers flying, proceeded to quilt three rows while standing right in front of us. She passed it around for us to see and also handed out sheets of tips for us.

Her final words were, "Remember, you are simply stitching layers together in a way that is uniquely yours. There are no mistakes, only happy accidents. Relax!"

The four of us went off to the dining hall chatting about the demo and excited to try some of the tips. Dee was at the table with our other couples, chatting amiably. I have to say that the service on this ship was first rate. We were served efficiently but not made to feel rushed. By the time we'd finished dessert and coffee, I was definitely relaxed.

Then we passed Laurie and Mike Lambert as we exited the dining room. He made eye contact boldly; she didn't. This guy was starting to irritate me.

Thirteen

"We can't do this by ourselves," Dee said thoughtfully. "Not if we're going to take this guy down without giving Laurie up as well. The first thing we need to do is call a meeting with the girls. I also think you should probably reach out to Gabe." Before I could object, she raised a hand. "Hey, I'm not saying he should come down here. But he might know someone who's in Miami or nearby who could nab this guy quietly when we land back in Fort Lauderdale."

"Wow." I grinned at her. "That's an amazingly sensible plan, Dee. You came up with that so fast!"

She nodded proudly. "I have my moments. So *you* can text everybody to come to our room."

One by one they answered back in the affirmative. Not one of them asked why and that gave me a warm fuzzy feeling. They trusted me.

And now the game was afoot. Oh dear did I just say that?

We moved our stuff around the room to try to fit everyone in as comfortably as possible. Within half an hour, the team was assembled.

I explained as simply as I could the situation as it was developing.

"One of our quilt instructors, Laurie Lambert, has asked for our help. It seems that her husband, Mike, is laundering money for some gang back in Florida. It's small time compared to most. But Laurie is getting scared of being caught with him and has asked us to find a way to get him picked up, in other words to make it stop, without her being implicated. Having said that, this probably isn't the first cruise they've done this sort of thing on and she's definitely helping him get away with it. So we'll have to see how this plays out."

Oddly, I think some of our past adventures have toughened the girls up. They scarcely blinked.

"So what do you need from us?" Queenie asked.

"My thinking is that our best help is to watch the guy. Try to get any incriminating evidence on him and then we're going to turn him over when we get back to Fort Lauderdale." I took a breath. "I'm going to call Gabe and see if there's an FBI agent anywhere around here that might be able to supervise when we land. We're going to help Laurie because she's a fellow quilter in trouble but I honestly don't want Gabe dashing to the rescue."

There were nods of understanding. We are an independent group of females.

"We're not going to do shifts like we did before when we were watching the drug dealers in town. All you have to do is keep an eye out for this guy." I held up my phone to show the picture. "You may as well also know that Ginny Hamilton, one of the quilting instructors, is a good friend of Laurie's and is also trying to help her. She sent the picture.

I'll text it to all of you. Obviously, you don't want anyone to notice you looking at it if you see him."

Dee summarized. "Basically, we want you to go about your business but if you see this guy, note the time and place, get a picture if anything looks off, and let us know." She grinned and added, "we're not going to give you a code but please don't send a text that says, 'Just saw Mike L. with bag of money' or anything stupid, okay?"

Shelby blurted out, "This is so cool. I didn't get in on the last investigation."

While I applauded her enthusiasm, it scared me a little. I gave her a serious look. "Remember, safety first. Do not put yourself in this guy's way."

She sobered up and nodded vigorously. "Of course, got it."

Dee added, "You should know that Lambert already has his eye on Miranda. If you see him anywhere near her, you may need to step in. He hasn't done anything stupid yet but we don't need to give him the chance, either."

I nodded. I wouldn't have said anything about that but it was true.

"One more thing. Tomorrow we'll be in Nassau. It would be real easy for Lambert to meet up someone there so this may be our best shot at getting something on him."

After they were gone, I made the call to Gabe, reluctantly. I had to balance the fact that I didn't want to make a big fuss over this and have him think I was sticking my nose in where it didn't belong against what would happen if he found out after the fact. Better to be in front of this, I decided.

"Hey babe." My husband's deep voice sent a delicious shiver through me.

"Hi honey."

"Is everything all right?"

"Sure. Well, sort of. I need to ask your advice on something."

"Okay." I could now hear the suspicion in his voice.

I tried to state the facts calmly like it was no big deal. My husband was way too smart to fall for that.

"I don't have to tell you that this is nothing you or the girls should be involved in at all. Good God, Miranda, money laundering? In international waters?" He huffed into the phone.

"I know. But she's a fellow quilter," I said softly.

"No, she's the wife of a small time crook who might well be in it with him for all you know."

I sighed. "Okay, you're not wrong. But I still would like you to reach out to someone in Florida who could take this guy in when we land without getting Laurie implicated. She's terrified that the men he works for will find out she snitched."

He breathed out slowly. "I'll make a call. But if there's not an agent available, I'm coming down there."

I heard a ruckus in the background. "Yes, Harry, I told her." He came back to me. "You can imagine how Harry feels about this."

I smiled in spite of myself. "Yes. Go ahead and tell him he was right. This cruise may not have been a good idea." Then I added, "Gabe, please don't come down here. I'm sure this won't be a big deal."

"We'll see."

"Love you," I replied brightly.

"Love you too." He grumbled, then clicked off.

I smiled. Okay, he was mad but not mad enough to hang up without saying he loved me. I could work with that.

Fourteen

Cruise Day 4 (Nassau)

The next morning I had a text from Gabe's old friend, Tom Gibbons, who happened to be in Miami for a conference and said he would be in touch.

I laughed out loud. Tom is a great guy who is also slightly envious of Gabe's happily-married status. I know for a fact that every time Gabe speaks with him he tells him to give me a hug for him. Gabe always says "no." Tom has mentioned from time to time that if I ever get sick of Gabe, I should give him a call. I think we probably both know that's not going to happen but it's flattering. Gabe would not be happy that I was working with Tom in any way, shape or form—without him nearby.

Tom's call came as Dee and I were having breakfast with the other girls in the buffet so I had to keep my response simple.

"Hey, Miranda, how's my favorite girl?"

"Hello, Tom," I said quietly.

"I sense you're not in a position to talk?"

"Right. Can I call you back in about fifteen?"

"Tell you what. I'll call you back in twenty. How's that?"

"Excellent. Thanks."

"Always my pleasure." Click.

Dee looked at me suspiciously. "What the heck was that?"

The others stopped eating and gave me their full attention, too.

I flashed the "not now" look. "It was TOM."

Confusion on all faces. I would have to elaborate. "Gabe's friend from work, Tom."

Understanding dawned, looks were exchanged, and eating quickly resumed.

"He's going to call back." I nodded significantly.

When we finished, Dee and I told the team we'd coordinate with them later since we weren't landing in Nassau until noon. We hurried back to our room

When he called, we both jumped. I put him on speaker but kept the volume low.

"Miranda, I don't know how a woman can go on a *quilting* cruise and get herself involved with a guy like this Lambert," He said seriously.

"It's not my fault," I said defensively. "His wife asked for our help."

"'Our help?' Oh Lord, don't tell me you have the other girls with you."

"Of course, it's a quilting cruise. The Cutler Quilt Guild #1 is here in force except for Brittany."

Diane waved a hand at me and pointed to herself.

"And Diane's here."

"Perfect," he replied with no small amount of sarcasm. "So listen. I did a little research. The Miami office has become aware of a crew operating out of Miami that's done a great job of staying off the radar by using small local operators like your guy. Any idea what he's doing on your cruise?"

I looked at Dee. "Dee thinks its money laundering. He's playing $500 slots and seems to have a pile of redemption tickets in front on him every time we see him."

He sighed. "That's classic, all right. You girls need to keep your distance. This gang uses small timers like Lambert to clean the money in exchange for keeping a bit of it. He'll stay low key. He won't have a ticket for more than $700 or so, nothing that would attract attention or require the casino to report it."

Dee was beaming. I rolled my eyes.

"Do you have any info other than his name?

"I have a picture."

Diane threw her arms up in a lightbulb moment and grabbed my schedule off the desk. She read fast and pointed frantically to Laurie's introductory bio.

"Okay Tom, Laurie, his wife, is one of our quilt instructors and the onboard guide says she and her husband live in Hollywood, Florida."

"That's a decent start. Now you and your team can keep an eye open but do not put yourself in this guy's way, okay? Bring whatever you can get to me and I'll take care of it. We might be able to flip him into turning over the bigger outfit if we don't spook him. And remember, although this guy is not a real pro, he could still be dangerous."

"Got it. We'll just keep our eyes open."

"Good girl. If anything happens to you, Gabe will kill me."

"I'll be careful."

"Do that." Tom clicked off.

Nothing much had really changed but I felt much better having Tom at my back, our back. I could tell Dee did too. We gathered our stuff for an afternoon in Nassau. Dee put on her bathing suit and covered it with a t-shirt and wrap-around skirt.

She caught my puzzled look. She grinned. "Ready for anything."

I had no intentions of getting wet so I stayed with light slacks and a top. Between us, we had hats, sunglasses, bug spray, wallets and big empty tote bags for the things we were likely to buy at the famous Straw Market.

Then we went on deck and watched as the ship pulled into Nassau. The tall buildings of the Atlantis Resort off to the left towered over the gorgeous setting. I had been surprised to read that there were almost a quarter of a million people in Nassau. As we disembarked, we were faced with racks of scooters and rows of taxis.

Suddenly Dee grabbed my arm. I followed the direction of her gaze and saw Mike Lambert renting a scooter.

As soon as he took off, Dee raced toward a taxi.

She jumped in and I followed, not having much choice since she had me by the arm. "Follow that scooter." She ordered.

The driver smiled, a toothy grin that lit up his face. "I wait a long time for 'dis."

We shot out of the parking lot area and took off after the scooter. It went straight down the street a few blocks and turned into the Atlantis Casino parking lot.

Our cabbie was clearly disappointed. "Well, dat was too easy, mun."

He cheered up considerably when Dee slipped him a twenty.

There weren't a lot of people at the entrance so we took our time following Lambert inside. We certainly didn't want him to look around and see us.

Not surprisingly, he was already out of sight in the massive casino area by the time we got inside. I was momentarily distracted by the glass Chihuly sculptures in the place. Ever since I saw the first one of his pieces, they have fascinated me. I have travelled several hours in different directions (Pittsburgh and Philly) to catch any exhibit which features these astonishing art creations. They are simply spectacular. I grabbed a couple of photos to send to Gabe who knew about my fascination with Chihuly.

After we spent fifteen minutes wandering around looking (ostensibly) for Lambert while taking in the sculptures, Dee tapped my shoulder. She pointed toward the high stakes area.

We casually moved in that direction. No sign of Lambert.

"We can check later." She whispered and pointed to a sign for the Aquarium and Lagoon areas. We both love aquariums, always have.

She wiggled her eyebrows at me. "Maybe he likes fish."

"Sure." I chuckled. "We should totally check it out."

For the next hour or so, we meandered happily through the marine exhibits.

The big surprise of the day came when Dee pulled off her t-shirt, stepped out of her shorts and flip flops, handed the pile to me, and jumped onto the water slide that went down through a nurse and reef shark lagoon. She had her arms folded tight across her chest as she flew down the clear slide. It was, no doubt, thrilling to see the big predators coming to check you out, to judge by Dee's open mouth and big eyes.

Yes, I got a picture which I took from the safety of a viewing platform.

As had already happened several times on this trip, we suddenly realized time was getting away from us and hurried back through the casino.

We stopped at a few machines; they're irresistible. As we approached the exit, Dee stopped and stepped back into me.

"Yeow. What is wrong with you? I'm wearing sandals here." I groused, rubbing my foot.

"It's Lambert," She whispered.

We moved to one side and watched as he recovered his scooter, loaded a green duffle in front of him, and took off before we stepped out and hailed another taxi.

We told the driver to head back toward the harbor as we scanned both sides of the road. We ask him to slow down as we drove past a turnoff and saw the blue scooter parked. Dee pretended to be fascinated by the cigarette boats at the water's edge and the palm trees. She asked our driver to circle back once and go slow.

Lambert was talking to a guy down at the water's edge by the boats. We bobbed up and down trying to get a better look while Dee snapped pictures.

Our driver wasn't happy about this. "Dey de fast boats for bringing in de drugs, ladies, you don't got to be messin' around 'ere. I take you to de Straw Market for some nice shoppin', yeah?"

"That would be great," I said enthusiastically and we turned around and headed back towards town again.

A red scooter whizzed past us and a hand raised in a wave. We looked at each other.

"Was that?" Dee asked, wide-eyed.

"Good Lord, I hope not."

We took our time going through the market and soon had almost filled our totes with t-shirt, purses, and other goodies too cheap to resist. When we got thirsty, we found a small café nearby and settled in.

She pulled out her phone. Many of the photos were blurry thanks to our moving taxi. I told Dee one of them was pretty good but, frankly, it wasn't really. You certainly couldn't identify anyone from it.

"Good job," I whispered.

Suddenly, Judy and Shelby appeared. "Hey girls. Mind if we join you?"

We pulled up a couple of chairs. After they ordered their drinks and snacks, Shelby whispered excitedly, "We saw the guy. We were just walking along, taking pictures of the water, you know, when there he was." She wiggled her eyebrows dramatically. "He was carrying a kind of duffle bag."

"Wow."

She held up her phone. "See?"

What I saw was a picture of a green duffle bag. I tried not to chuckle, I really did. Judy was desperately holding back giggles herself.

"What?" Shelby looked at the picture, then at us.

Dee, never one to soft soap anyone, blurted out, "Well it's not really any good, is it? I mean that could belong to anyone. He's not in the picture, honey."

"Oh." She looked so crestfallen we all fell silent.

We walked back toward the ship and saw Queenie and Sarah just ahead of us, preparing to reboard.

We called out and they waited for us.

Queenie gave me a wink. I knew better by now than to hope for much.

We all seemed to head toward our room by consensus. The ship was fairly deserted as most of those on board wanted to spend every hour possible on the island.

Once inside, Sarah told us their tale. They too had seen Lambert on the beach on their way to the Atlantis casino. It was, indeed, Queenie and Sarah who zipped past us. It took me a moment to absorb the fact that Sarah was driving.

When they saw Lambert and the man, they pulled over and walked down.

"You did what?" I gasped.

Sarah chuckled. "We did a 'two drunk old ladies' act. I pointed and said, "Look Myra, that's one of those speedy boats from Magnum PI."

Queenie piped up. "And I said, 'it is not, you old fool.'"

"So the man turned toward us and said, 'You're right, ma'am, that's a cigarette boat just like on TV.'"

Sarah took over again. "So I said, 'take my picture with it.'"

"Then I acted like I was too drunk or too stupid to take a good shot so the man took a picture of Sarah with the boat for us." Queenie grinned.

"Ohmigod," Dee said.

Queenie nodded. "I know. And while he and Lambert were helping Sarah, I kept swinging my phone around, taking pictures." She proudly held up her phone and there they were, clear as a bell, with the duffle on the sand between them.

We all cheered and high-fived. Queenie sent me the photo and I sent it off to Tom with an explanation.

"That's a good day, ladies." I yawned. "I don't know about anyone else but I think we deserve a rest before dinner."

"Works for me." Queenie stood. "Tell you what. Why don't we all skip dessert and meet at the Pie Shop for pie and ice cream, say around 8?"

"We deserve it!" Shelby chirped and everyone laughed.

After another delicious meal, we joined up and had to choose the kind of pie we wanted. I won't elaborate (drool factor) but we did share and exchange the kinds of pie. My fave was the coconut lime custard, actually, with coconut sherbet on the side. Oops.

Before I turned in, I texted Gabe.

Nassau today, the Atlantis was wonderful. Love you. I added several pics of the Chihuly sculptures and then I added the picture of Dee on the slide, just to make sure Gabe knew we weren't all work and no play.

He texted back at once with a laughing face. *Harry loves pic of Dee.* A moment later, *But he wants you to know he's still not happy with you.*

So I replied, *I'm used to that. As long as you are happy with me, I'm good.*

I am and I will prove it to you when you come home. Counting the hours.

I know I'm a soft touch but I got a little misty. I took a deep breath and reminded myself we were more than halfway there.

Fifteen

Cruise Day 5 (Coco Cay)

Since we weren't arriving at our next stop until noon, the quilting bee was scheduled for 9AM. From our texting, I knew that Sarah and Queenie had signed up for it and would be there; Judy and Shelby might stop by to watch for a bit but were essentially going to do a major walk around to all the shops surrounding the atrium. I hadn't signed up to participate but wanted to have a look at the quilting bee myself and Dee was curious since she'd never seen one before either.

After breakfast, we made our way to the big theater lounge where the bee was set up. It was impressive. Twelve long quilting frames stretched end to end across the space. Brightly colored quilt tops, batt, and backing were stretched over each frame. There were needles and baskets of thread and thimbles on side tables.

There were also about a hundred quilters milling around, getting supplies. I spotted Allison's white hair and saw her with Jennifer laughing and smiling in the mix.

After a few minutes, Allison blew a whistle.

"Good morning. We're so happy to see such a wonderful turnout. I want you to know that the quilts you are working on today will be bound and auctioned off with the proceeds going to the Fort Lauderdale Children's Hospital. I know that volunteer work and philanthropy are close to the hearts of all quilters. We'd like to work until about 11AM which will give you all time to prepare for our arrival in Coco Cay. If some of you want to stay longer, one of us will stay with you. So please settle in at a quilt that you like and let's go!"

It was impressive to see how quickly these quilters seemed to know what they were doing. I was glad I hadn't joined even though I do hand quilt; I was nowhere near the speed or caliber of these quilters. Sarah and Queenie were, of course, right at home and chatting cheerfully to the ladies on either side of them as they nimbly worked the quilt. There were no men, in case you were wondering. I believe that the male quilters I have met are more drawn to the drafting and technical skills of quilting than the hand quilting aspect. I could be wrong; maybe they just couldn't face being in here so badly outnumbered.

We watched in fascination, walking back and forth behind them, as fingers flew across the fabric. Allison and Jennifer moved from frame to frame as well, making suggestions or offering help where needed. I heard them encourage each quilter to add their own initials to the edges of the quilt or inside corner of a block.

Dee gave me a look that said she was ready to go. Checking my watch, I saw that it was after ten. She wanted to stop at the pharmacy onboard and take another look at a scarf in one of the shops.

We had our beach bags ready to go when the ship arrived at Coco Cay, a private island owned by the cruise line. It has a big water park, all kinds of water sports, restaurants and such. Yet it's only about a mile long. You can choose between lots of noisy activities and finding yourself a spot on the beach. The beach, being dry land, sounded good to me.

This time we both wore our suits although our intentions were different.   Dee and I decided to split up for the day. While we are typically together a good bit, the enforced closeness of sharing the cabin and the ship overall made it an easy mutual decision. She took off towards the "action" while I grabbed my beach bag. I was happily surprised that by walking away from the main area, I found a tiny secluded beach surrounded by rocks, all for myself. As much as I love my home, we don't have beaches, we have mountains.

Maybe going off on my own was a foolish thing to do but, for heaven's sake, it was a small island with a ship full of people all around. I doubted that I'd be alone for long. I spread out my towel and closed my eyes, lulled by the sound of the surf. White sand, aquamarine water, warm sun.

I dozed contentedly until I realized that my sunscreen was wearing off. Then I roused myself to lather up and grabbed my book. But my eyes kept going to the water. A million shades of blue, it was crystal clear nearer the beach. I took a picture with my phone even though I knew it would never do justice to the amazing scene in front of me.

Suddenly, a shadow fell over me and I looked up.

Mike Lambert smiled down at me, then flopped into the sand.

"Mrs. Downing." He said quietly.

"Mr. Lambert." I managed to sound affronted instead of scared, I think. With my left hand, I started digging through my bag for my whistle.

"Maybe I might call you Miranda since we keep meeting."

"Mrs. Downing's fine."

He nodded and kept smiling as he spoke without looking at me. "I got a lot of friends in a lot of places." He pulled out his phone and showed me the picture I had sent Tom the day before. He sighed. "You really need to stay out of my business."

"Go away, Mr. Lambert. Or I'll…"

He chuckled. "You'll what?"

I pulled out my whistle and held it up for him to see.

A tall brunette, beach bag in hand, towel thrown over her shoulder, approached us.

"Hey there. Do you mind if I join you? It's getting a bit crowded on this side."

"Not at all," I squeaked, lowering the whistle to one side.

"Excellent." She moved to a spot on my other side and proceeded to spread her towel.

Lambert's dark eyes were angry. He leaned in toward my ear and whispered, "This is your one and only warning. Mind your own business."

He stood, brushed the sand off his shorts, and walked away.

The man sure knew how to ruin a mood. I realized I had been holding my breath and blew it out in a rush.

The woman was lying flat, sunglasses in place. Without moving, she asked, "That guy isn't yours, is he?"

"Dear God no, he's a creep."

I heard a deep chuckle. "That's what I thought and I've only known him three seconds." She sighed. "Men. They never know when to take a hint that a girl wants to be alone, do they?"

"Apparently not." I closed my eyes and gathered myself. As soon as I stopped shaking, I wished my rescuer a good afternoon, gathered my stuff, and walked slowly back towards the main area.

I spotted Laurie and Ginny at the outside cocktail bar. I slid onto a stool next to Laurie. The pretty bartender came over and I said, "I'll have whatever she's having."

At that, Laurie looked at me and her face fell.

"What are you doing, you can't be seen with me! What if Mike…"

I raised a hand. "That ship has sailed, excuse the pun. He just came up to me on the beach and threatened me."

"Ohmigod."

Ginny leaned past her to stare at me, wide-eyed. "I'm so sorry, Miranda. We had no business getting you involved."

My drink came and I took a good gulp. It was quite tasty until the alcohol hit my stomach and bounced back up.

"Well, we are where we are. I've been wondering how he plans to get the duffle bag back on the boat and then off in Ft. Lauderdale. We have to go through customs and all."

Laurie's face now went pink.

"The duffle bag doesn't go on the boat. He transfers the money into my tote bag. They don't search staff. My stuff goes into the duffle and he takes it back on board."

I stared at her. "It's almost as if you've done this before."

She leaned over and whispered, "When we land in Fort Lauderdale, the money is inside my backup sewing machine. It's a fake; it's hollow."

"Wow. That's really clever." I took one more sip of my drink, left a $10 bill on the bar, and stood up.

"One more thing. The FBI will be waiting for him. If, for any reason, he doesn't show up there or the money's not there, a lot of people will be wondering who tipped him off."

I walked slowly back toward the ship. I'd had enough relaxing island time for one day. What I'd said to Laurie and Ginny was to make sure they didn't tip Lambert off. But someone already had. That picture kept appearing in front of my eyes. Who sent it back to Lambert and so fast? It was frightening. I had to let Tom know someone in his office was leaking straight back to the money launderers.

First, I texted Dee to let her know I was going back. She replied that she was with Judy and would see me for dinner. Tonight was the Captain's Dinner and we got to dress up.

I took a long hot shower and a nap and my spirits started to rise. I decided not to mention my run in with Lambert to anyone else. They could only worry and watch me closer which I didn't need.

I kept wondering how to get in touch with Tom. I didn't really want to but finally decided my best option was to call Gabe.

I explained what had happened. He listened in silence. "So basically you need to let Tom know there's a mole in his unit without letting the mole know you called."

"Exactly."

He sighed. "You know I'm not happy about this, Miranda. But I can reach out to Tom off channel and fill him in—only if you promise to be really careful for the next couple of days."

"I will." I said with relief. "Thank you."

"Yep. Love you."

"You too."

That was all I could do for now. I made a trip to the casino and played slots for an hour after looking around carefully to make sure Lambert wasn't there. I came out about even but it was relaxing. Can't believe that there's a Monty Python machine! Run away!

Sixteen

I could well imagine the scene at Tom's office when Gabe had made his call. He would have been angry and, well, embarrassed. Later, when it was all over, Gabe filled me in on the details…

Tom Gibbons stood up and went directly into the Managing Director's office. He had known Jeff Darton for thirty years and, if there was one person he knew he could trust, it was Jeff. As soon as he told Jeff what had happened, Jeff's face looked much like his own, flushed and angry. Together, they went over every person who had been in the office for the 24 hours after Tom had received the photo.

After a few minutes, Jeff admitted to Tom that he had suspicions about a guy who had recently transferred in from New York. He was young, married and had two small kids. Moving to Miami didn't seem to make much sense since it wasn't a promotion.

Tom moved directly to his file. John Roberts, three years with the Bureau.

"What do you want to do?"

Jeff grinned. "What we always do, bluff."

Tom nodded.

They found that John was out of the office and didn't want to alert him so they waited. He showed up about 3:30 and they quickly moved him into Jeff's office.

He took a seat while Tom lounged against the door behind him. That clearly made him nervous as his only way out was effectively blocked.

"What's up, boss?"

Jeff shoved a copy of the photo across the desk. "The jig is up, John."

"I don't know what you mean." The young man shifted in his seat.

"Are you telling me you didn't see this picture yesterday?"

"I don't think so."

"You sure about that?"

"Uh, maybe I did but it wasn't my case."

"Can I see your phone?"

"Sure." The young man handed over his phone. Too easily. Tom and Jeff exchanged glances.

Tom spoke up. "Your personal phone."

"Oh, that's not here. It's locked in my desk like it's supposed to be when I'm on duty."

"So get it."

When John stood and went through the door, Tom followed him. He glanced nervously behind him. Tom smiled. "Wouldn't want you to accidentally push a wrong button or drop it, would we?"

A few minutes later, they were back with Jeff.

The man scrolled through the texts and then sighed as he showed John the screen.

"Care to explain this?"

"How did you?"

Jeff smiled. "Tech background. In your deleted texts. Nothing's ever really gone anymore."

The picture was there, no message, simply texted to a number.

"Hey why don't we give this a call?"

"No, don't, please. You don't understand. My wife is Cuban. They tracked down her abuela; they know where she lives. They said they'd kill her if I didn't make this move and do what they asked. They promised no one would get hurt."

Tom and Jeff looked at each other.

"Why didn't you tell us?"

John shook his head.

Jeff closed his eyes for a moment. "I accept your resignation. Clear your desk."

The young man's eyes widened. He composed himself. "Thank you, sir." He straightened his tie and stood.

"Not so fast," Jeff added.

Fear came back into the young man's face.

"Here's the deal. You can go next door and tell Agent Jameson everything you know, dates, names, all of it."

Roberts started to protest.

Jeff stood. "Or you can go directly into custody and think about how long you'll be in prison."

The agent's shoulders sagged. "Okay."

Jeff softened a tiny bit. "If you do a good job, we will relocate you and your family."

Tom opened the door for Roberts. "You know, it's a relief, really. Now that I am of no use to them, they will leave me and my family alone. At least they'll be safe." He walked through with a nod.

Tom and Jeff were quiet for a minute.

Then Jeff shrugged. "Hope springs eternal."

I felt sorry for the young man when I heard the story. But it seemed as if our problem of the leak was solved.

Seventeen

When I returned to our room, Dee was sound asleep on her bed so I grabbed my tote bag and went back out. I found a deck chair in the shade a few feet from our door. As I pulled my paperback out, a card flew onto the deck. It was a crisp cream with black formal printing.

SPECIAL AGENT JANET LOWRY
FEDERAL BUREAU OF INVESTIGATIONS
MIAMI FLORIDA

with a cell phone number.

On the back, she had written, *"Call me if you need me."*

I was flabbergasted. The brunette on the beach, had to be. Well, well…

There was to be no reading for me. I sat there for half an hour, then it was time to get dressed so I went in and woke Dee up.

Did I tell her about the agent right away? No. She was so excited about the Captain's Dinner, it didn't seem right to insert this issue, once again, into the fun.

She chattered the whole way to the dining room about how much fun she had on Coco Cay so all I had to do was nod and smile. When we got to our table, our tablemates and we complemented each other on our outfits. I don't dress up much but it is fun once in a while to feel like Cinderella at the ball.

The Captain was as tall and handsome as you could want him to be. He introduced himself, told a few funny stories, and encouraged us all to have a good time.

The dinner finished up with all the lights turned off as the servers came through with flaming baked alaskas. I've never seen anything like that before; it was also quite tasty.

Then the music started and the tables were moved aside for dancing. I made my way over to Queenie's table and chatted with her and Sarah, then Judy and Shelby stopped by as well. Everyone was looking quite pink and healthy. Everyone was smiling and I intended to keep it that way.

Since we were short on fellas, several gentlemen offered us a dance. I surprised everyone by accepting. My partner was a tall, silver-haired gent who reminded me, of course, of my Gabe and we had a lovely conversation as we danced. He mentioned that his wife was on crutches and he pointed her out at their table. I saw the crutches beside her and threw her a little wave and she waved back.

"I'm sorry." I whispered to my partner.

He smiled. "Don't be." He chuckled. "I told her not to go down the big water slide but did she listen? Nooooo…."

I breathed out in relief. "Broken ankle?"

"Nah, just a bad sprain. But she is sorry to miss the dancing. By the time we get home, she'll be able to lose the crutches."

"Thank heaven."

He looked down at me curiously. "You're right, of course, it could have been a lot worse." Then he twirled me around until I was gasping for air. We whirled past Dee and Shelby out on the floor with their dance partners. Talk about taking my mind off my troubles!

He escorted me back to my chair and kissed my hand. "Lovely to meet you, Miranda."

"You too, Charles." I smiled up at him. It's always refreshing to know there are still gentlemen out there.

I kept my eye out for a tall brunette but, if she was there, she was doing a great job of blending in.

Queenie and I took our drinks and went out on the deck. We walked a bit and then settled in deck chairs to watch the sunset over the water. It was so peaceful.

When it was all but dark, we each headed back to our rooms. It had been a long day and fresh air makes me sleepy.

I was almost to our room when a dark shadow appeared in front of me. I could see his smile in the moonlight. He simply pointed his hand at me in the shape of a gun and then he was gone.

I opened the door with trembling fingers. I was afraid and I hate being afraid. It makes me angry.

Dee wasn't back yet. My first thought was to be worried but then I looked at my watch. It was 9:30. For heaven's sake, I chided myself, you're not her mother.

I washed my face with cold water and got into my pjs. I took a water bottle from our frig and drank half of it down.

I texted Gabe that all was well. It was, at the moment. But, before long, this bastard was going down.

Eighteen

Cruise Day 6 (More Water)

Dee's intentions were good, as always, in securing a room with no windows, given that we were just above sea level on this deck. But I still expected the sun to come in and wake me. I was getting used to checking my phone for the time.

She was sleeping so I threw on some clothes and went down for breakfast. Queenie and Sarah, our early risers, were there but Judy and Shelby were sleeping in. No surprise there, I could only imagine how late they'd been up after the dinner.

Dee came in as we were finishing up.

"So what demos are you going to today, Miranda?" Queenie asked.

"Oh dear, I totally forgot to look at the schedule." I felt guilty that quilting had taken a back seat to Lambert.

She reached into her ever-present tote bag and handed it to me. "Here you go."

She and Sarah went off to take a walk before the first quilt demo at 10.

Today's choices were:

10:00 AM Quilt As You Go! Jennifer Myers

12:30 PM English Paper Piecing Allison Hopewell

2:00 PM   Small Quilted Presents Virginia Hamilton
5:00 PM Circles in Quilting Laurie Lambert

I was pretty good at Quilt As You Go and didn't want to go to Laurie's demo so that left two. I had seen English Paper Piecing but never tried it and, although we made small items in guild, I was curious to see what Ginny would present as presents. I had a feeling it would motivate me when I got home to start my Christmas projects. It's never too early!

So I'd be tied up from basically 12:30 to 3:00 with time for maybe a quick snack in between.

"What are you doing this morning?" I asked Dee.

She shrugged. "To be honest, I'm not very motivated. Maybe I'll just walk around the ship a bit and then find a deck chair."

"Do you want company?"

"Sure." She grinned. "Everything's more exciting when you're along."

"I hope not." I too felt a tad weary today. But it was our last full day and I didn't want to arrive home feeling like I hadn't taken full advantage of the ship's many offerings.

We walked around the shops, stopped for a coffee, found a large hot tub that was actually empty and raced back to our room to change and then hurried back and jumped in. It was so relaxing that I may have dozed off because suddenly Dee was smacking me on the arm.

"Hey sleeping beauty. It's 12:00."

"Oh Lord." I got out and put on my cover up. "Thanks, sweetie, catch you later." She waved a hand and leaned back in the tub.

The Paper Piecing demo was clearly not the most popular one on the cruise. There were maybe 50 or so of us gathered toward the front of the lounge.

Allison came out with an armload of materials and gave us a smile. "Good morning. I admire your bravery. We who are about to…and all that."

Laughter ensued.

She waved a hand. "I know. English Paper Piecing. The first thing I have to ask is, how many of you have ever tried this?"

Maybe a dozen hands went up.

"And how many of those think that getting the paper out of the pieces is, well, a royal pain and the reason you're not doing more of it?"

The same hands went up.

She chuckled. "I couldn't agree with you more. But we're going to fix that. Now, to start, why do this at all? Well, paper piecing is supposed to make shapes easier to handle. You see a lot of hexagons and such. It can be difficult to get sharp points and edges simply sewing the pieces together. Let's get started."

She held up paper templates in several shapes and talked about sewing the papers inside them. It was a matter of basting folded edges over the templates. She quickly basted a hexagon into place and held it up.

"The beauty of this is that I now have a firm piece rather than a limp piece of fabric to work with. When you do sew these pieces together, you want to leave the paper templates in as long as possible, simply removing the pieces after you have sewn any given area of a larger project.

"Now the tricky part! First let me say that using copy or print paper is not a good idea. So how about using a leave-in stabilizer?" She held up what looked like a stiff interfacing fabric.

I blinked; I had never thought of that. Now it seemed obvious.

She grinned at the looks on our faces. "Right, now here's another option." She poured her water bottle into a small bowl and took the hexagon she had just made and dunked it. A small chorus of gasps escaped our group.

"It's fine, I promise." She pulled out the dripping hexagon and nimble pulled the soggy paper template out.

"You see? If you wet the paper template in place, it's easy to pull out. Now you will probably want to press the pieces dry but you'd have to press the sewn pieces at some point anyway."

She went on to describe various projects made of pieced shapes but I was kind of fixated on how simple it was to remove the templates—once you knew how.

She got a brisk round of applause and, as had happened before, a small group surrounded her when she finished. I dashed for the door, knowing that I had half an hour or less before Ginny Hamilton's group.

By now, I knew where the nearest snack bar was located so I grabbed a granola bar and iced tea and hurried back to the lounge.

The idea of making gifts seemed to have appealed to more people and this group was twice the size of the other. A familiar red-tipped hand shot up and wiggled at me and I settled in beside Queenie and Sarah.

We make quite a few small items at guild but we were all kind of excited to see if Ginny could show us some quick and easy new ones.

As soon as she took her place behind the table at the front, it was clear that something was wrong. She simply didn't look well.

She took a drink from her water bottle and seemed to pull herself together. She managed a smile and greeted us warmly.

Although much of what she presented, such as burrito-style pillowcases, was familiar to us, she did show us how to make some lovely quilted ornaments. That triggered an urge in me to make some for our "kids," my daughter Zoey and her husband Michael and Gabe's son Kevin and his wife Terry.

These young couples were starting to create their own holiday traditions and the idea of handmade ornaments for their trees felt like it was right up my alley, so to speak.

Belatedly, I realized I should have taken notes all week on the things that appealed to me. Sigh.

Pulling my attention back to Ginny, I realized she was running through the steps to make tote bags out of charm packs, which I had seen before but never done, and giving a few tips on making potholders look more professional. She whipped up a drawstring gift sack like it was easy so I was impressed. She finished up by showing us a lovely pillow made from what is called a "candy ring," four pieced curves which together form a circle. She had appliqued a Christmas ring onto a white background and added a red bow.

We gave her a warm round of appreciative applause, especially when she said that there were handouts covering the basics we could pick up on the way out. This time, the three of us made our way through the crowd to grab one of those.

I headed back to the room for a quick rest and intended to spend the rest of the day and evening experiencing the ship. Tomorrow afternoon, we'd be home!

When I had undertaken this cruise, a week had seemed endless. Now I was surprised to find that it was almost over. There were areas of the ship I hadn't even seen yet!

I was about to text Dee to catch up with her when my phone rang. The ID said it was Ginny. She hadn't looked well earlier so I answered quickly. "Hello?"

"Oh Miranda, I can't find Laurie! She's not answering her phone and I knocked on the door of their room, I don't know what to do."

A shiver ran down my spine. He wouldn't dare…would he? I fought off a moment of dizziness as my worst nightmare of going overboard flew through my head.

I took a breath. "Okay, let's stay calm. She has a demo group in about an hour. If she doesn't show up for that, we have a problem."

She took a moment to compose herself. "Okay, you're right. Maybe she'll show up and it'll be fine." A last sob escaped. "Thanks Miranda."

"It's all right. Now let's touch base after that, okay?'

"Great. I'll call you." She clicked off.

Dee meandered in shortly thereafter from another jazzercise class and my rest period was over. We looked over a map of the ship to see what we might have missed. Besides a couple of restaurants, there was actually a small stationery/book shop that I couldn't believe I hadn't visited, an interesting candy shop that Dee couldn't believe she'd missed, and we both realized there was a whole lounge show with dancers and singers after dinner.

Dee showered and changed and off we went. A couple of purchases (history magazines and licorice) later, it was dinner time, our last dinner with our table friends. We were having dessert when I realized guiltily that I hadn't checked my phone. I had been enjoying myself too much to think about Ginny and Laurie.

No message. What? I looked at Dee and she gave me a puzzled glance back. I finished quickly, said goodbye to the rest of the table, and excused myself. I waited in the sitting area outside until she came out, a few minutes later.

I had filled her in on Ginny's concerns about Laurie earlier. "There's no word from Ginny."

Her frown deepened. "So we need to find out if she showed up for the 5:00. Why don't you text Queenie and see if any of the girls were going?"

A few seconds later, the answer came. "I didn't go but Sarah did. She says, no Laurie so they cancelled."

Dee and I exchanged worried glances. I didn't want to say it out loud but that never stopped Dee.

"Laurie and Ginny are now both missing, right?"

Nineteen

It was now time to let Dee know about Lowry.

"Dee, did I mention that there's an FBI agent on the ship?"

Her big eyes got bigger. "No, you did not."

"Right. Well, I think we should call her."

"Wow. This is awesome." She nodded, her curls shaking. "Make the call."

I dug the business card out and plugged in the number. It rang only once.

"Yes?"

"Agent Lowry, this is Miranda Hathaway. I have reason to believe that both Laurie Lambert and Ginny Hamilton are missing."

I heard a sigh. "Now I know why Director Gibbons asked me to keep an eye on you. You don't miss much, do you?" She paused. "I decided to isolate Mrs. Lambert this morning. She insisted all day that Ms. Hamilton be protected so I picked her up as well. They are both safe."

"Oh." I looked at Dee. "Okay then."

"Was there anything else?"

"No, thank you."

The phone clicked off.

"You heard?"

"Yeah." Dee took a breath. "What happens now?"

I thought about it. "If you're Mike Lambert and your wife, who knows all about your criminal activity, is suddenly missing on a cruise ship, what would you think?"

She replied, "Something has gone wrong and I'm likely to be arrested when this ship docks."

"Exactly. So what are your choices?"

She gave it a few seconds of thought. "As I see it, my only choice is to get off this ship before it docks."

I raised an eyebrow.

She grinned. "Well, a helicopter would be nice but would draw a good bit of attention." She shook her head. "Nah, has to be another boat, there you go."

We did a bit of research. The ship would slow to a virtual crawl tonight off the coast before docking tomorrow.

Dee narrowed her eyes. "We need to find him."

"What about Agent Lowry?"

That chin went up. "Well, she can't be everywhere, can she? I would think she'd appreciate the backup."

She quickly texted the girls to keep an eye open and report any sightings. We started moving around the ship where there were large numbers of people. If he was half as smart as he thought he was, he'd want to be visible if he thought Laurie was missing.

The music was starting in the big theater lounge and we gravitated that way. Separating, we moved around the edges of the crowd, scanning for a tall, dark figure. When we came together, we shook our heads.

Next, we went to the casino, moving straight toward the high limit blackjack tables. I was truly surprised that he wasn't there.

My phone vibrated. "Deck Five, Carousel Bar."

I showed the phone to Dee. We moved as one toward the stairs through the atrium. Then we went down the stairs on the other side and entered the bar.

He didn't look up when we came in but continued talking to a couple sitting next to him.

I tapped him on the shoulder. "Hi, Mike," I opened in a friendly tone.

"Mrs. Downing." He nodded politely but his eyes let me know that he was not happy to see me.

"And this is Diane." I waved at my trusty cohort. "We were looking for Laurie. Just wanted to ask her one last question about her quilting demo. Do you know where she is?"

He shook his head and a glimmer of humor came into his face. "No, sorry, I don't, but I bet she's with that friend of hers. Ginny, isn't it?"

I managed to keep a smile on my face.

Dee took the lead. She stepped into his space. "If you see her, tell her we're looking for her, okay?"

"Sure." He picked up his drink and showed us his back.

When we were outside the bar, Dee gave an elaborate shiver. "He doesn't know where she is so I guess that's good. But, oohh, what a creep. How does anyone ever marry a guy like that?"

"I hear you." I shook my head. "A lot of times, guys like that come across as charming until they have you. It's truly sad how many women, especially those who don't attract a lot of guys, fall for that act."

"I get it. And I suppose Laurie's afraid to try to divorce him."

"I believe it's just gotten worse and worse. If she tried to now, she'd be a threat to him and never feel safe." I shook my head. "Let's find a place to sit down and think."

The place we found just happened to be the ice cream bar. As we enjoyed our last hot fudge sundaes, we pondered in silence, only the sound of ice cream being eaten filling the air.

As we finished up, I sighed. "Assemble the team."

Twenty

"So, basically, you want surveillance on Lambert straight through until tomorrow when we dock." Queenie said calmly.

Miranda sighed. "I know. I'm sorry. I guess we are doing shifts, after all."

"I wish I'd brought more gear." Sarah replied thoughtfully. We all knew what she meant. Sarah's sister, Harriet, had put together quite a collection of stun guns and was not afraid to use them. In fact, she had once accidentally taken Sarah out with one. So it was rather surprising that Sarah had started carrying one with her. She swore she heard Harriet's voice in her head telling her which one would be needed. I knew she missed it but was also grateful that she probably figured she couldn't get it through customs.

Judy, ever our organizer, moved us along. "Okay, people, we need shifts." She checked the time. "It's after 9 now."

Then she asked, "Do you want to do this in twos or singles?"

"I think it would be best in twos in case something happens." I answered.

"Right. First team up has to go find the guy, checking on the bar on five first, and text us. What say, two hours on, starting now?"

We all nodded our agreement.

Sarah and Queenie were early to bed girls so they took that first shift and stay until midnight. Shelby had no problem with the 12-2AM and Judy, somewhat less enthusiastically, decided to stay with her. Dee and I took 2-4AM and Sarah and Queenie, having had benefit of a couple of hours' sleep, volunteered to pick up the last shift of 4-6AM. Each team would text the next team with a status report. It was highly doubtful that Lambert would act after the early sunrise.

At 7AM, we all agreed to touch base and see where we were. My feeling was that he would make his move under cover of total darkness. I said a silent prayer that it would be on my shift so that none of my friends would get hurt.

Dee and I were no longer in the mood for the music so we walked around a bit and returned to our room. I know we were both waiting for a text that called us out to action. I did fall asleep somewhere around midnight and was stunned awake at 1:50AM by Shelby's report that all was quiet. She said Lambert had returned to his room and was still there. I replied and woke Dee.

We stepped out into the warm air. As we approached Lambert's room, Shelby stepped out of the shadows, stifling a yawn. She saluted and said she'd sent Judy off to sleep. I nodded my thanks and gave her a smile as she tread lightly away. Dee and I had each grabbed a coffee on our way from one of the 24-hour self-service kiosks.

We slipped around the corner and found deck chairs. I tried to sip coffee every few minutes to keep from dozing off and knew that Dee was doing the same.

It was about 3:15 when I heard a cabin door open. I touched Dee's arm and she nodded. We stood silently and slipped inside the deck door to the interior of the ship. Lambert, duffle in hand, came around the corner, moving stealthily past us toward the outside steps. He started down and we moved out and followed.

Deck six was the deck closest to the water with the lower numbers virtually being underwater. He moved to the rail. Once we realized it was this deck he was heading for, we moved inside so he wouldn't see us and watched through the window.

He tied a rope to the railing and I could hear the dim sound of a throttling motor boat. We were now only a few miles off Florida, the cruise ship holding in place until tomorrow. This was his best chance.

Still, it was fascinating to watch him tie a rope to the duffle and toss it over. A moment later, the rope went taut again. Was he really going to shimmy down that rope?

Not on my watch. I opened the door and ran smack into a fire extinguisher box. Geez, that hurt. I grunted.

He turned at the noise and saw me. "What the hell are *you* doing here?" He took a step toward me.

I couldn't even bring myself to say something inane like "I couldn't sleep." I just shook my head and backed away.

"Hope you're a good swimmer, lady." He grabbed my arm and pulled me toward the rail. I fought against my fear and slammed an elbow up and into his face.

"Ow. Damn." He loosened his grip just enough for me to turn and face him.

Dee came up behind him and grabbed his hand, pulling his thumb back. We had learned that in the self-defense class we had taken together. It really hurts, by the way. He went straight to his knees which is what is supposed to happen. Then she sprayed pepper spray in his face. He screamed and the tears started running down his face.

I pushed his other arm behind him as he doubled over and she whipped her new scarf out of her pocket and was trying to tie his hands as he struggled.

I pulled out my phone and pushed the speed dial number. I was stunned to hear the phone ring only a few feet away.

Suddenly, a tall shadow appeared and a female voice said, "It would have been good if you'd called a little sooner, Mrs. Downing." As Dee stepped aside, an arm went around Lambert's neck. I heard a click and saw silver steel gleaming in the dim light.

I took a breath. "You're right."

"I think we're about done here, Mike." She placed the hard metal of the gun against his neck. "In case you don't think this is real, my friend, I assure you it is and I know how to use it. Now you can let me cuff you quietly or you might have an awful accident. We can see how long it takes the sharks to smell your blood in the water."

He stopped struggling and let out a long sigh of a breath as tears wet his face.

"Okay, now call your friends off down there." She pushed him toward the rail and he waved the boat off.

"Good man. Now back on your knees."

She glanced over the side as the boat pulled away. She pulled out her phone and speed dialed. "Coast Guard 3134, this is FBI Lowry, 47259. The motor boat pulling away from the Voyager is white with red trim, two occupants. Intercept and detain. Thank you."

Her smile gleamed in the dim light as she pocketed the phone. "Are you okay, Mrs. Downing?"

I rubbed my head where it hit the box. "I'm fine, thanks.

She manhandled Lambert back inside and into a small office marked "Security." There were two ship's officers waiting. Unable to stand it, Dee moved forward and used her scarf to wipe the pepper spray tears off his face. He scowled at her and she pinched his cheek. The officers took him into another room.

Agent Lowry stayed with us. "Would you feel better if you saw the two other women?"

I didn't know about Dee but I sure would and I said so.

Lowry opened another side door and there they were, sound asleep on pallets.

When the door opened, both women jumped. Laurie blinked a couple of times and stared at the agent. "Is it over?"

Agent Lowry nodded. "Everything but the shouting. You may have to testify but we'll do our best to keep you out of it. Your husband is in custody." She stepped to one side. "And you have these ladies to thank."

I flushed. I realized that she had everything under control and had been one step ahead of us the whole time. It was a bit embarrassing. "But you could have handled it. You must have been tracking him."

Lowry chuckled and shook her head. "No ma'am. I was tracking *you*."

"Oh." I looked at Dee who was smiling from ear to ear.

Laurie started to cry. "Oh, Miranda. Thank you, thank you."

Ginny chimed in and there was quite the hug fest. The agent told me that Dee and I might need to give statements when we got back to shore. Then she let us go.

On the way back to our room, I texted the team to let them know it was over; details to follow. I made sure to let Queenie and Sarah know that they did not have the last surveillance shift.

"Hey, you still got some 'splaining to do." Dee glared at me. "When did you find out about her?"

"I know, Dee, I'm sorry. I found out she was on board right before the Captain's Dinner and I didn't want to ruin that night for you."

She grumbled a little, then said, "Okay then."

The bump on my head hurt a little but my heart was much lighter. I got back to our room and crawled back into bed. I guess Dee did the same; I was totally out.

I heard her stir around 7:30 and got up. I looked at the tousled head of my BFF. "Hey, in case I didn't say it last night, Watson, you were great out there. Pepper spray?"

She yawned and sat up. "Yeah, they sell little ones at the pharmacy on board if you can believe it. I figured better to be safe than sorry." She shrugged. "I got a new scarf out of it, too."

I smiled at her. "You're awesome."

She said solemnly but with a twinkle in her eye. "It's just what Watsons do."

Twenty-One

e joined our friends for one last buffet breakfast. Everyone was a bit subdued and a little weary, no surprise there. But they wanted details and I gave them as much as Agent Lowry had told me I could share.

Apparently, Tom had assigned Lowry to follow me. He was more concerned about her protecting me than capturing Lambert, she said. She had put several trackers on me and my stuff, including one in my phone. During the day, she was trying to be unobtrusive and simply checked my location periodically. At night, after she saw that I was safely in my room, an alarm would sound on her phone only if I (or the phone) left the room again. So her alarm went off when Dee and I moved out to follow Lambert.

I'm glad I didn't know beforehand, it would have made me uncomfortable.

I let Dee share the details of our early morning capture. If she dramatized it a bit, I let it go. She deserved to bask in the moment. I thanked everyone for their willingness to help and made a mental note to make sure Laurie knew that all six of our team were involved.

After breakfast, we all had to get our bags together and put them outside our rooms, tagged and ready to go. This was one aspect of cruising I liked. It beat the heck out of lugging your bags to and from hotels.

It may sound odd but the general quilter's roundtable gathering was at 10:00 and the five of us wanted to attend. Ending our cruise on a quilting note felt right. Dee opted for one last jazzercise class but the rest of us trooped down to the big lounge. Jennifer and Allison were beaming as more and more quilters came in to join. They sorted us into rounds of ten chairs for smaller groups before intending to chat with us all together.

What a joy to be amongst all these smiling faces! The five of us took a round and five others filled the rest of the chairs. We were given twenty minutes to talk about whatever we liked. The conversation started hesitantly about the demos on board but soon took off in other directions. When one of the other quilters casually dropped a remark about how belonging to a quilt group was like adopting a second family, the five of us all nodded as one. Then someone added that quilters are always people with big hearts and so being a member of a group means that they will share their joys and their sorrows. The ongoing theme of our little group was that quilters trust each other and they are always good people.

A small pang went through me. I wanted that to be true but I wondered.

When we rejoined the larger group, Jennifer announced that twelve quilts, an even dozen, had been completed by the quilting bee teams and congratulated everyone on a wonderful job. She then insisted on a round of applause which was enthusiastic. Then she asked everyone to fill out a brief questionnaire about the cruise.

"We're not going to ask you to name your favorite quilt instructor," she said with a grin, "but there are spaces for notes at the bottom and my name is spelled Myers, M-Y-E-R-S."

"Hey!" Allison popped up beside her. "And mine is Hopewell, thank you."

"Sure." Jennifer teasingly elbowed her to one side. - "However, we are asking for your feedback on the demos. You can help us make future cruises better by letting us know which topics interested you the most."

Allison handed out piles of sheets and pens and they were passed through the group.

After about ten minutes of letting everyone focus on those, she asked to have them passed back up to the front.

Jennifer continued, "Now, if those who were in groups for discussion would like to share any of the thoughts that came out of those, we'd love to hear them."

An awkward silence ensued and then Queenie, bless her little red head, raised her hand. Jennifer nodded.

"I think one thing we all agreed on was that being a member of a quilt group or guild is like taking on a second family, good and bad." She nodded firmly and sat down.

That got her some laughs and some applause.

Having broken the ice, several others stood and added their thoughts.

Finally, Jennifer and Allison stood together and thanked us all for coming and being such wonderful guests. They invited us back for the next quilting cruise at which point Allison waved a brochure.

"You're gonna love this one, ladies. In October, we'll be quilt cruising to…Alaska!

There were appreciative gasps and Dee elbowed me. I glared at her.

As we made our way to the gangplank for our final exit of the ship, Queenie came up beside me.

"So what do you think, Miranda, up for another cruise to Alaska?"

My mouth fell open, then I sighed loud enough for our whole team to hear.

"That would be a hard 'no.'"

As we say, leave 'em laughing when you go.

Twenty-Two

As we exited the ship, I saw no signs of Lambert or Lowry or any law enforcement. I assumed they were waiting until the passengers disembarked so they wouldn't scare them off cruising. What I did see was Tom Gibbons waiting off to one side, arms crossed. His face lit up when he saw us coming down the gangplank.

I had already explained that I might have to make a statement so when I waved the rest of the girls on, Queenie nodded her understanding. I gave each of them a quick hug and told them I'd see them at home. They had a plane to catch and I was not likely to be on it.

"Miranda!" He stood back and took a look at me. "You look radiant."

I'll bet I did after only a couple hours of sleep. "Thanks, Tom."

"Okay, you look like you want to go home with your friends but you will need to come with me for a bit.

He noticed Dee hovering at my elbow. "It's okay for you to go home, Diane, I don't think we'll need a statement from you."

Her face fell but she didn't move.

Tom leaned forward and whispered in my ear.

I in turn whispered in Dee's ear and she managed a smile and a nod. Then she hurried off to catch up with Queenie and the others.

Tom shook his head. He took my arm and we went out a door to a waiting black car.

"Uh, about my luggage?"

He grinned. "In the trunk, my dear."

My eyes widened. Okay, I was impressed. It's good to be law enforcement, sometimes.

He held the back passenger door for me and I slipped in. Gabe was waiting inside and a small sound simply came out of me.

He grinned and opened his arms. I flew into them. For the first time in a week, I truly felt safe. For the record, I did not cry. I might have misted up a little.

We talked all the way to the police building where my statement would be taken. Tom was good enough to let us be as he sat in the front with the driver. He even raised the window between the seats so we could have our privacy.

When the car stopped, I look at Gabe.

"It's okay, honey, we do this and then we go home. Harry has a lot to say to you."

He knew how to lighten the mood and make me smile, this guy.

Tom escorted me into an interrogation room and turned on a recording device. For the next half hour, he asked questions and I answered as best I could.

We came out to find Gabe waiting again.

"Where's Lambert?" I asked.

Tom hesitated, then answered. "He's actually in another building. There's procedural stuff and paperwork for the Ft. Lauderdale police to take custody and then turn him over to us." He lowered his voice. "I'd like to get him out of here, to be honest. I'm taking him back to DC with me."

Suddenly, I remembered my manners. "Thank you, Tom, for everything." I smiled. "Agent Lowry is really kick-ass, if you don't mind my saying so."

He chuckled. "That would be why I sent her." He added, "Now I know you're anxious to go, but how about I buy you lunch first?"

I was anxious but it felt churlish to refuse. I could wait another couple of hours. I nodded. "Is that okay with you, Gabe?'

"Sure. We're booked on a 5:00 flight."

Tom looked disappointed. "Oh, he's coming too?"

Gabe punched him in the arm and he shrugged.

He took us to a local place nearby and I was particularly grateful that it wasn't too dressy since I was in slacks and a top. We had a lovely time until Tom's phone went off. He frowned and excused himself.

When he re-settled, he leaned forward and said in a low tone, "Lambert is talking and he's saying this whole thing was Laurie's idea."

Oh no. I gave it a moment's thought. "Well, it's in his best interest to say that, isn't it?"

He nodded.

"Where is Laurie, by the way?"

"She made her statement and was released." He paused, then added thoughtfully, "Lambert also looked surprised when confronted with the fact that the duffle bag contained around $300k."

"What are you thinking?" Gabe asked.

Tom's eyes narrowed. "I suspect, at the least, that Laurie managed to squirrel with some of the laundered cash. Who's going to complain?"

A light went on. "Wait, Laurie said that her backup sewing machine was hollow."

Tom looked puzzled. "No it wasn't. We went through everything she had with a fine toothed comb before we let her go."

Oh. An idea started to form but before I could straighten it out to put it into words, Tom's phone chimed again.

"Damn." He stood and signaled to the waiter, handing over his credit card. "I think I should get back. You guys take your time. I'll leave the car to take you to the airport."

Then he was gone. We looked at each other.

"I know it's frustrating to feel like you don't have all the pieces, sweetheart, but 99% of police work is like that. Let's go home."

Twenty-Three

We were waiting at the gate when a local news break came on the TV in front of us. GANG SUSPECT SHOT DEAD. I gasped. Gabe sighed.

His phone chirped. He listened, muttered a few things, then clicked off.

"Tell me." I said quietly.

"Lambert was shot while being transferred into Tom's custody. Tom wanted him out of there before there was any chance of the Jiminez gang finding out where he was." He shrugged. "Looks like there was more than one mole and they weren't fast enough."

"My God."

He went silent.

"Now what are you thinking?"

I squeezed his hand. "Forgive me, love, but I am thinking that I don't want to think about anything but going home."

He smiled. "Sounds like a plan."

======

"Harry!" I threw open the door and there he sat, trying for an annoyed look. But I picked him up and heard the purr as I buried my face in his soft fur. Tears unexpectedly tickled my lashes. "Oh Harry, I'm home."

He muttered a little something which I chose to interpret as "good to see you too, mom" and then struggled to get free. I let him go. Cuddling was a great affront to his personal dignity and the boy could only be expected to put up with so much. Then he naturally headed for the kibble. Emotional outbursts always make Harry hungry.

Gabe followed through the door with my bags and set them in the hallway. Then he put his arms around me and held me for a good few minutes until I settled down.

I ignored the bags and got us each a glass of wine and we took to our recliners to decompress before bed.

Being as sensitive as he is, Gabe waited for me to bring up the subject. I didn't. A lot of emotions were fighting inside me and I felt that it would be a day or two until they sorted themselves out.

When we went to bed, I didn't think I'd fall asleep easily but I did. And it was good to wake to see the sun coming in the windows. Funny the things you miss when you're away.

It was Monday and I should have gone into the library and started catching up. But I had texted Lucy last night and she was happy to cover one more day. I don't know what I'd do without that girl. At the same time, I knew my inbox would be overflowing.

Still, I had a pancake breakfast prepared by my wonderful husband, did some laundry, and was not at all surprised to hear the back door open around lunchtime.

"Come on in, Dee." I called from the living room where I was dusting a bit.

"Glad to be home?"

"You betcha? You?"

She shrugged, then grinned. "Well, Mark is awfully nice to me after I've been away." The grin faded. "Of course the house was a mess."

"I hear that." Gabe was tidier than Mark but somehow never seemed to see dust and he doesn't do bathrooms.

We took a seat at the kitchen table and I managed to scrape together soup and sandwiches for our lunch.

"So where is the big guy?"

"He had a call from a client and went to Philly."

She frowned.

"I said it was okay, honey, I don't mind the peace and quiet really. Back to work tomorrow and all." I chuckled. "I do believe we're all safe now."

She nodded. "Okay so tell me everything that happened after we left."

"Well, essentially, I made my statement, Tom bought u lunch, and we flew home."

Her mouth settled into a pout. "You're leaving out all the good parts."

She saw the look on my face and immediately relented. "You don't have to talk about it if you don't want to, really."

I put down my sandwich. "You deserve to know because you helped take Lambert into custody." I swallowed. "The first odd thing was that Tom felt that some of the laundered money was missing."

It took Dee less than a second. "So Laurie had it in the hollow sewing machine?"

I nodded. "That's what I thought. But Tom said they checked all her stuff." Since it was Dee, I paused for effect and raised an eyebrow. "Neither of her machines was hollow."

"What? Why would she lie?" Her eyes widened, then she smiled. "She switched machines with Ginny."

"You are quick. It took me a little longer to figure that out."

"Wow. It's not like anybody's gonna complain so she's gonna get away with it."

"Looks like." I paused, "But there's more."

She leaned forward, all ears.

"Lambert was shot dead before they could get him out of that facility. Tom was going to take him back to DC. He wasn't sure he'd gotten the contact in the department that was tipping off the drug dealers."

"Ohmigod." Without thinking, she added, "Poor Laurie."

I remained quiet..

She gasped. "You don't think…"

"I actually texted Tom this morning. He said he had her watched all the way until she boarded her flight. She never even took her phone out of her bag."

"Maybe she bought a throwaway?"

I shook my head. "Never went near a store or a kiosk."

Dee took a drink of her iced tea.

We looked at each other and neither of us wanted to say what we were thinking.

We ate some but not all of our lunch and then Dee announced that she had to run, hair appointment. That made me realize I could use a cut myself. I called and made an appointment for the weekend.

Before she left, she asked, "Miranda, are you going to tell Queenie and the others about, you know, Laurie and Ginny?"

That was the question. "I'm not sure. So please keep this to yourself."

She gave me a quick hug. "Of course."

One thing I love about Dee, who is not always the most lovable person, is that she really gets me.

Twenty-Four

The clink of my keys as I unlocked the library doors gave me a little jolt of happiness. I stepped inside and took a good long look around. Had it only been ten days?

I made coffee in the break room and, carrying a hot cup, walked slowly up the steps to my office.

Even the sight of my paper-covered desk couldn't wipe the smile off my face. Out the window behind my desk, Cutler was coming to life. I knew most of the people walking the street to work. I knew most of the kids playing in the schoolyard and making their way to day camp. I closed my eyes for a moment and one word appeared: HOME.

I hard Lucy barreling up the steps, early as usual, and the sight of her red hair and freckled face was welcome.

"I'm so glad you're back." She came around the desk and threw her arms around me and I returned the hug warmly.

"Yet I had every confidence in your ability to keep things running while I was gone." I said and I meant it. She was a hard-working and talented library administrator. I'd love it if she took over for me when I retired but I knew that she had a lot of life ahead to deal with—husband, children, who knows? So I try to appreciate her while we are here together.

"So what did I miss?" I waved her into the chair in front of my desk.

She opened her iPad and I knew we were going to be here for a while.

We managed to get the library open to the public at 10 and then, as one of our trusty volunteers manned the front desk, we went back to my office and kept going. At this point, I was taking notes and making lists.

Lucy made a trip to a deli for lunch and we worked straight through. By 3PM, she indicated that we'd gotten through most of it, or at least designated priorities.

"Wow. Okay, let me work on the deposits first and then I'll turn them over to you. After that, emails, I guess and then mail."

She nodded. "The new shipment of books is in the corner of the break room. Do you want me to start unpacking them until you're ready for me?"

"Sounds like a plan." I took a breath and a sip of iced tea. "Lucy, in case I don't say it enough, you're incredible."

Her fair skin turned a mottled pink. "Just doing my job."

"Well, plan a vacation, will you?"

She smiled. "Actually, I am. I thought I'd wait till the end of the week to break it to you."

Looking at my desk, I agreed. "Probably a good idea."

We worked diligently until 5 and then called it a day. Yes, I could have probably stayed until midnight to clear my desk. But one of the things I love about library work is that very little of it is urgent!

Gabe was home and I smelled Italian when I came through the door. He took a look at my face and told me to relax, dinner would be ready in half an hour. He got no argument from me.

We talked easily as we ate his lasagna, which is better than mine, and the fresh bread he'd picked up at the bakery.

"How was the trip to Philly?" I asked. He'd gotten in late last night and neither of us was up for much of a chat.

He shrugged. "Not as well as I had hoped."

I waited. If he wanted to tell me more, he would. So much of Gabe's work is confidential, I've learned not to pry.

"How was your first day back?"

Change of subject acknowledged, I gave him the highlights.

"Your face lights up when you talk about your work." He grinned. "Who would ever imagine that library work was so interesting."

"Probably anyone who loves books." I showed him the new bestseller Lucy had handed me as we left. "First dibs."

"So what do you want to do after dinner?"

I hesitated. "I know we don't do it often but could we go for a walk?"

"Around town?"

I nodded.

"Sure. That won't take long."

"Very funny."

Harry appeared at my feet. He chattered, then looked at me with narrowed eyes.

"No, Harry, I'm not going away again. I said for a walk. Probably no more than an hour if we go slow."

He watched me carefully for another few seconds then left the room.

Gabe shook his head. "I do believe we have the weirdest cat on the planet."

"I'm not sure he knows he's a cat." I said with a grin.

I strolled arm-in-arm with my husband around Main Street. As I expected, most of those still out and about at this hour, walking dogs or window shopping, stopped to say hello and ask about my trip. We stopped by the Ryans' workshop and Gabe proudly pointed out some of the custom woodworking he'd helped with. It seemed like only a few months ago that this space was a dusty, failing shoe shop before we found out that Mr. Ryan hated that business but made wonderful little bird houses.

With my Gabe's support and encouragement and now with the enthusiastic participation of several Ryan sons, the burgeoning business has its own web site. They not only make whimsical houses but can make a custom mini of someone's home. Queenie proudly sported a replica of her Victorian in her yard.

I was, of course, delighted to have Gabe engage in any activity that didn't involve carrying a gun.

I took a look at the windows of a few shops that I hadn't been by for a while and made a note to stop in during open hours. It's always nice to patronize local. The big mall just outside of town was great for major shopping or making a day of it but, in the smaller shops, you could stop and chat for a bit.

We made it home to find Harry waiting patiently (or not) in his recliner in the living room. Taking a hint, Gave played a taped Jeopardy and the three of us engaged in a spirited contest. We mostly let Harry win. If he's not always right, he's usually the loudest.

Twenty-Five

Six Days Later

When I got home from work on the following Monday, the table was set for three. I went into the kitchen and found Gabe chatting with Tom Gibbons.

"Miranda!" Tom hugged me, a few seconds too long, until Gabe forcefully pushed him back. I shook my head with a smile.

"This is an unexpected pleasure."

Tom looked at Gabe. "You didn't tell her I was coming?"

Gabe shook his head. "She would have fretted about it all day."

"Good point."

My patience was straining to the breaking point as we had a lovely dinner of meatloaf and mashed potatoes with apple pie for dessert. In this instance, Gabe had wisely stopped by Sylvia's and picked up the food then gone to the bakery for a fresh pie.

As Gabe cleared the table, Tom looked across at me. "I have some news related to the Lambert case. I didn't want to share it over the phone. This is your chance to tell me you want to hear it or you'd simply rather let it go."

I did think about it; I did.

I got up and got a glass of water and waited until Gabe sat back down with us.

"Hit me with it."

Tom seemed to gather his thoughts for a minute. "I hardly know where to begin. I'm sure it has occurred to you that Virginia Hamilton was working with Laurie."

I nodded. It sure had.

"We pieced together her actions that day. Here's what we figured out happened." He began, "Virginia Hamilton stayed on board and watched until Mike Lambert and Laurie were off the ship.

"She waited until the last wave of staff was leaving and then she joined the group. She carried her two sewing machines through customs and gathered her other luggage.

"She hopped into a private car and gave the driver directions, keeping her purse, tote bag, and one sewing machine in the back seat with her.

"Over the next hour, she made quick stops at three banks. Then she went onto the airport and checked her sewing machines and suitcase.

"At the airport, she bought a burner phone at a self-service kiosk, made one call, and threw it into a trash bin.

"Then she got on a plane to go home.

"Laurie Lambert made her statement, collected her luggage and two sewing machines, and went directly to the airport. Agent Lowry reported this to me and was then instructed to return to the office."

"You followed the wrong woman." I said without thinking.

He nodded. "We sure did. What we didn't know at the time is that Virginia and Laurie are half-sisters."

I did not see that coming. I opened my mouth and closed it. I said nothing; there was clearly more.

Tom took a drink of his wine and let that sink in.

"They have the same mother, different fathers. Their mother had some…issues. When she had Virginia, the baby was adopted by a lovely family. Two years later, when she had Laurie, the child went into foster care. She didn't have much luck and was in six different homes before she turned 18 and aged out. Her life was," he swallowed, "much more difficult than Virginia's."

I felt my throat thicken. How unfair did life have to be? I found my voice. "But Ginny told me she had known Laurie about ten years, I think. Did she just lie?"

He shook his head. "No, she actually didn't. They never knew about each other until they met at some quilting thing, got to talking, and did a bit of research. Then they figured it out."

"So when Laurie realized she had gotten herself into trouble…"

"She called her big sister." He looked away for a minute. "They were looking for an answer to Laurie's problem when they realized you had booked onto the cruise. Virginia, of course, knew who you were. They needed a way to turn Lambert over to us without the drug cartel suspecting that Laurie had ratted them out."

Gabe inhaled sharply and I felt the anger rising in him. I wasn't affected quite the same. I had already figured out that I had been used and had a little more time to get used to it.

"And it worked." I said softly.

He smiled rather sadly at me. "It did. But there was a second part to their plan. After Lambert was in custody, Laurie wanted him dead."

"Was he going to reveal that she was really the brains behind this scheme of money laundering on the cruise ships?" Gabe asked.

"I'm not totally sure." Tom answered. "He certainly was trying to pin at least some of the blame on her." He sighed. "We weren't paying much attention to what he said because we were expecting to interview him later on tape and in greater detail. At that point, he just seemed to be rambling." He took another drink. "Then he was killed."

I inhaled sharply. Gabe looked down at the table.

Tom went on, "Before you ask, no, Laurie did not show up to claim the body. He had an aunt in Fort Lauderdale and she made the arrangements."

"My God, that's cold." I heard myself say without thinking.

He cleared his throat. "She had the body cremated and was going to have it interred in the family plot near Hollywood. No service."

"You're just a font of good news." Gabe swore and ran a hand through his thick white hair.

"I'm sorry. Believe me. There's one more thing."

We waited in silence.

"Lambert was killed on Sunday. On Wednesday, Laurie filed a $1 million dollar insurance claim on him.

Tears filled my eyes and I closed them for a moment.

Gabe moved his chair and put his arm around my shoulders.

"I'm sorry, Miranda. There was no easy way to break all this to you."

I composed myself after I saw the pained look on his face. "It was all for nothing then, wasn't it, Tom? Lambert's dead, Laurie's rich, and the guys behind the scheme are carrying on exactly as before."

He heard the defeat in my voice. "Not exactly." He looked at me kindly. "This is how it works, Miranda. We try to break one link in the chain. What you and your girls did was give the agency a good bit of information that they can follow up on." He counted off on his fingers. "Someone on that ship had to be aware of what Lambert was doing, The Atlantis in Nassau seems to be involved in the money laundering as well; the guy driving the cigarette boat; the boat registration and owner; the realization that there are moles in the law enforcement organization."

He took a breath. "There's probably more, too. Agents will be working on this for months. You never know what bit of info will be the one that leads to the big score."

He opened his briefcase. "This isn't much but it's something."

He handed me one of those fancy certificates, signed by the Director of the FBI. It was awarded to Cutler Quilt Guild #1 in recognition of services provided to the agency.

"Thanks, Tom" I managed a small smile. I could see the girls going nuts over this.

Tom left shortly after that.

I might have cried a little and Gabe knew me well enough to let me be. What kind of a world did we live in where it seemed like the bad guys were winning? I had been played by fellow quilters. That was going to leave a scar.

Harry was a little put out that we weren't playing Jeopardy but he sat in his recliner next to mine anyway. At one point, he laid a paw on my leg. I patted his head.

"I'm okay, Harry." I said quietly.

But I wasn't really. Tom had said that no group is entirely good or bad. All police aren't good; all murderers are not bad. There is no 100%. I heard him. But quilters were supposed to be different. That's the way I felt.

I went to bed early but I still heard Gabe come in. He immediately knew I was awake and laid his arm across the pillow. I laid my head on his shoulder and he stroked my hair until I fell asleep.

Twenty-Six

Gabe and I walked in silence to quilt guild on Saturday. It was our charity work meeting wherein once a month we made things for a local group. At this point, word had spread enough that Queenie usually had to choose from several requests to decide our projects.

Gabe walked straight back through to the long arm machine where projects were always stacked up, waiting to be quilted. It was his favorite part of quilting and the least favorite for the rest of us except Queenie so she was always glad to have his help with the backlog.

We started chatting and Queenie tinkled her scissors against the side of the table to get our attention.

"Okay ladies, come to order, please. As you know, this is our monthly charity project Saturday so we need to get right to it. I think you'll like this one. Today we have a request from the hospital for bibs and burp pads for newborns."

A chorus of "oohhs" erupted. Queenie smiled. "These are pretty straightforward flip and sew but you all get to choose your fabrics. I have a stack right here, along with two bib patterns. I figure we'll have two cutters, three on the machines, and one finisher to put the Velcro fasteners on the bibs. Let's have two machines on bibs to start and one on burp pads and then maybe we'll switch after break."

She didn't really have to assign the tasks any further than that; everyone knew what they wanted to do and probably what everyone else would do. Sarah would do the finishing, she always did, and Shelby, our least experienced sewer, would cut. It always worked itself out and sometimes we switched jobs at break.

We worked along steadily until Queenie called time and brought out the coffee and donuts. She got Gabe to come and join us. After a few minutes, I went into my tote bag and pulled out the certificate.

"Ladies, your attention, please." I said in an imitation of Queenie. Everyone chuckled except Queenie who looked puzzled.

"Tom Gibbons dropped this off at my house." I held it up and read it. There was a round of applause and I presented it to Queenie, who was now smiling too.

All of a sudden it hit me that she might want to put it out front here or even display it in the window. For reasons only Gabe knew, I didn't think I could bear looking at it every week.

She held it for a moment and then looked at me. "Well, this is lovely. I think I'm going to put it above my desk in the back. If any of you want to show it off, you go right ahead. But I'm not putting it out here where all of Cutler will know about it in fifteen minutes and come in here wanting to know the whole story." She waved a beautifully manicured hand. "They'll know what we want them to know."

I sighed in relief.

I planned on following that advice myself. I had learned some hard lessons this time around; my faith in all quilters being good people had been, well, dented if not broken.

The Cutler quilters would know what I wanted them to know. I couldn't unknow these hard truths myself; I wish I could. But I guess I'm not a "misery loves company" kind of person. There was a wonderful innocence in this quilt guild and I'll be damned if someone like Laurie Lambert was going to destroy that.

I looked at Gabe and he smiled at me. Sometimes I wish he wasn't so good at reading my mind.

We finished up our charity work and applauded the totals when we finished, as we always did.

Everything was as it should be at Cutler Quilt Guild #1 and it was going to stay that way—at least for now.

Epilogue

I started going through the Monday mail at the Library when a bright card caught my eye.

It showed a beautiful island beach and two women, holding up pretty drinks with umbrellas. The back read,

"Thanks Miranda, for everything. We couldn't have done it without you."

It was unsigned.

Authors' Note:

In case you are wondering what happened to the appearance of Miranda's supposed sister in the Epilogue at the end of *The Quilting Queen*, don't be concerned. That situation is still developing but we decided Miranda deserved a vacation first.

The Baby Quilt is still in the works. Thank you for your continued support. It means the world to us.

Mary and Beth

Mary Devlin Lynch lives in the Bronx, New York City. She's a notorious multitasker, combining quilting and writing with reading two or three books, all at the same time. She also runs her husband's business.

Beth Devlin-Keune lives in Florida. With her Administration of Justice degree, her insight has been helpful in several of the books. She is also a voracious reader and watches as many sports as is humanly possible.

<u>Other Books by the Devlin Sisters</u>

The Witherspoon Adventures:

Beautiful Disaster (Magee), Book 1

Burnt Roses (Melissa), with Beth Devlin-Keune, Book 2

Before Everafter (Madison), Book 3

Relative Unknown (Cari), Book 4

Cayden and Cat Adventures:

The Wright Move, Book 1

The Wright One, Book 2

The Wright Woman, Book 3

Meredith Abbott Adventures:

Lying for a Living: Meredith Abbott's Adventures in Hollywood, Book 1

Dying for a Headline: Meredith Abbott's Adventures in England, Book 2

A Hollywood Designer Adventure:

Sophie by Design

Skylar Kincaid, Editor:

The Dame in the Diamonds

Miranda Hathaway Adventures:
  The Quilt Ripper, Book 1
  The Missing Quilter, Book 2
  The Quilt Show Caper, Book 3
      with Beth Devlin-Keune
  The Quilter's Secret, Book 4
  A Quilt to Die For, Book 5
  The Quilter's Christmas Surprises, Book 6
  The Quilters Push Back, Book 7
  The Quilting Queen, Book 8

Darcy Garrett Art Shop Mystery
  Stormscapes
  Darcy's Snowscapes
  Irelandscapes: A Killing in Kilkenny